DEATH AT AN ENGLISH WEDDING

SARA ROSETT

McGuffin Ink

DEATH AT AN ENGLISH WEDDING
Book Seven in the *Murder on Location* series
Published by McGuffin Ink

Copyright © 2017 by Sara Rosett
First Paperback Edition: June 2017
ISBN: 978-0-9988431-2-4

Cover Design: Alchemy Book Covers

❀ Created with Vellum

"Next to being married, a girl likes to be crossed in love a little now and then. It is something to think of."

— PRIDE AND PREJUDICE

CHAPTER 1

THREE WEEKS UNTIL THE WEDDING

"*S*eating charts are enough to drive someone to murder." I stared at the large sheet of poster board covered in sticky notes that rested on my kitchen table. I flicked another sticky note against my fingertips. I'd written the name of the latest RSVP, "Toby Wintergarden and guest" on it, but I had no idea where to put it on the circles that covered the poster board, which represented the tables for our wedding guests.

"Then I'll set this coffee down here," Alex said, "and back away quietly." He took a few steps backward, but he was smiling so I knew he wasn't serious about escaping.

I seized the thick mug with my free hand and inhaled the rich aroma of dark roast. "Exactly what I needed." I reached out my other hand—sticky note and all—toward Alex. "Don't leave. I need you to help me figure out where to put Toby." I waved the sticky note on my finger.

Alex pointed to an open space. "Why not here, beside Freya?"

"Because that table is documentary people," I said, referring to the crew from the Jane Austen documentary that Alex and I had worked for during the last year. "Toby won't know any of them. Shouldn't we put him at a table with at least one familiar face?"

Alex bent his dark head over the poster board. "Sure, that sounds good. What are the other options?"

"We don't have any other options. That's why I'm so frustrated." I took a long sip of the coffee then frowned at the geometrical designs on the paper. "The rest of the tables are packed. We have a few open seats, but it's like a giant jigsaw puzzle, except there isn't an image on the box to look at. I can't move Toby without moving his 'plus one' as well, which means that he can't go anywhere else."

"Then let's ask Malcolm to add another table and reshuffle."

I twisted around in the chair and looked at him. "We can't do that."

"Why not?"

"We just can't."

Alex pulled out a chair and sat beside me. "Kate, this isn't like you. What's going on?"

I tapped my mug, considering how to word my reservations. "I don't want to ask for another table."

Alex pointed his coffee toward the schematic of tables and chairs. "Think of it as a logistical problem on a shoot. You've sorted out things much worse than this. Remember the Garden Shed Debacle?" Alex asked, shifting into a falsetto British accent to imitate Elise, our producer on the project. She always referred to the incident with a shudder and somehow managed to convey capital letters when she spoke about it. He returned to his normal voice as he said, "When that storm blew up out of nowhere you had to move something like half the cast and crew into that little shed. You got it done, and we were able to get what we needed on film that day."

Alex was right. I could shift and sort people, lights, and generators, no problem. I could wheedle, plead, and threaten as needed when it came to pulling off a location shoot. "But that's work. The wedding venue is a gift. I don't want to ask for more."

Lady Stone and her husband, Sir Harold, had offered to host our wedding at their stately home, Parkview Hall. The country manor was open to the public for tours during the summer and also hosted various weddings and events throughout the year. Adding our wedding to the schedule free of charge and covering the cost of the venue was their gift to us.

It seemed a perfect solution to the question of where we would get married. Alex and I had spent quite a bit of our time during the last year filming at Parkview in our role as location scouts. We'd lived in the nearby village of Nether Woodsmoor in two cottages. Getting married at Parkview meant our local friends could come to the wedding, and most of our extended family were thrilled with the idea of traveling to England for a wedding at a beautiful country manor.

"Beatrice won't mind an extra table," Alex said, referring to Lady Stone by her first name. She didn't stand on ceremony and preferred to be addressed informally.

"Malcolm will. He won't say anything, but he won't have to." Malcolm Stewart had a way of expressing disapproval without saying a word. It was something to do with a long silence combined with a slight pinching of his lips as if he was working hard to keep his words inside. Malcolm was the head of event coordination at Parkview. I knew Beatrice thought she was doing us a favor by assigning him to personally handle our wedding, but I would much rather have worked with Parkview's more junior publicity assistant, Ella Tewkesbury. I'd met Ella when I stayed at Parkview during one of their country house weekend parties and gotten to know her well.

Alex took a sip of his own coffee then angled the seating schematic so he could see it better. "Okay, what can we do?" He stared at the paper for a few moments then waved his hand over the diagram. "Take off all of these sticky notes and start over?"

"No! That would be ludicrous."

My voice must have been a little sharp because he gave me a concerned look. "Kidding. I was kidding."

"I know it's crazy to get so worked up about these little details," I said. "But you try dealing with them for days on end and also having to work with a finicky person like Malcolm and see how you react."

Alex hitched his chair closer. I watched his dark chocolate-colored eyes as his gaze tracked back and forth across the poster board. Finally, he leaned back. "I've got it. Let's get rid of assigned seating."

For a second I couldn't actually respond. I finally said, "We can't do that. That's worse than starting over."

"Why can't we do it?"

"That's not how it's done here." The note with Toby's name was still stuck to my fingers, and I used the heel of that hand to rub my forehead. "I'm starting to sound like Malcolm. That's his favorite thing to say—*that's not how it's done*—and in that exact condescending tone. 'This is England,'" I said, hitting on his stuffy tone. "'This is an English wedding. Certain traditions must be observed.' That's an exact quote from Malcolm, by the way. He'd be perfect as a snooty butler in a period drama."

"I agree that he may have missed his calling, but that's not the point. What Malcolm thinks is irrelevant. English tradition—as great as it is—shouldn't be the focal point of our wedding. We're American. No one expects us to follow tradition. Why can't we have open seating if we want? There's not some sort of rule book written in stone."

"I do believe there is—Parkview's event contract. And Malcolm is quite adept at quoting from it, but..." I pressed my fingertips against the adhesive of the sticky note then pulled them away. "I could probably convince him to have open seating for everyone else during the reception as long as we kept a seating plan for the head table." I stared at the chart for a moment. Perhaps I was letting Malcolm's expectations overrule what would work for Alex and me. The absence of place cards shouldn't be this big of a deal. "Yes, let's do it. You're right. I've been letting Malcolm push me around, and I shouldn't do that."

I pressed the sticky note with Toby's name into the white margin of the diagram, pressing down with a little more force than was necessary. "Okay, the seating is set. Now I have to convince Malcolm that it won't cause the stars to come out of alignment."

"I'll take care of that," Alex said.

"Great. I'll write you a note." I grabbed a pen. When I'd first met Alex, I'd been surprised to find the dashboard in his car covered in sticky notes. I'd never understood how he could use the random bits of paper to keep track of his appointments, but I learned that the system worked for him.

"Don't need one," he said.

"You're sure?"

"Yes, I'll go by there tomorrow on my way to photograph Dale Court."

I dropped the pen and turned to him. "They're interested?" I asked, immediately diverted from wedding arrangements.

"Yep, asked if they could have my first available opening."

I pushed back my chair so that I could face Alex. "That's wonderful. You know what this means, don't you? We're in double digits." Alex and I had opened an online directory of stately homes for location scouts. With Dale Court, Elegant Locations would have ten country homes with full profiles of each location: multiple photos of each interior room with measurements as well as extensive photos of the grounds. Even outbuildings like stables and gatehouses were included. Our goal over the summer had been to convince owners to list their properties with us. Eventually we would have a full membership site, a one-stop shop for location scouts searching for everything from elegant drawing rooms perfect for Victorian dinner parties to gargoyle-encrusted manors on lonely moors ready for a Heathcliff.

"I think a celebration is in order." Alex held out his hand, pulled me to my feet, and dropped a quick kiss on my mouth. "Let's take a break."

I looked back to the kitchen table. Beyond the poster board, my laptop glowed with a pre-wedding checklist. I was on item three of twenty-seven. "I have so much to do. Weddings don't plan themselves, you know."

He leaned back, but still held me in his arms. "I could plan this wedding in a few minutes. A quick trip to the Register Office, and we're done."

I shook my head. "Tempting, but we can't."

"I'd even do flowers," he added quickly.

"I think we've passed the point of no return. Half the guests are flying in from out of the country. They'd be pretty disappointed to arrive and discover the wedding already took place."

"We could show them jolly old England. That should be enough, right?"

"I don't think that would cut it, especially with my mom."

"Surely she has a few long-lost British cousins. She can look them up."

Alex and I had flown back to California and visited my mom after we announced our engagement to our family and friends. "He is good looking," my mom had whispered on the way to the car at the airport, "but since you seem so determined to snag a man in England, you should have at least aimed for one with a title." Alex had pretended not to hear her and worked to charm her with his good manners. He didn't interrupt her convoluted stories about multitudes of unknown people distantly related to us that she had discovered as she researched her family tree. And Alex's ability to carry two suitcases at once up the stairs to her condo—"so manly and strong" Mom had said—had impressed her so much that she had him rearranging her living room furniture. Alex's endless patience as he moved the couch and chairs back and forth had won her over completely.

"Genealogy will take a back seat to the wedding," I said. "She's been planning it since the day I was born."

"Okay, I know when to cut my losses," Alex said. "Manor house wedding it is, then." He looked over my shoulder and checked his watch. "You can take a half-hour break, can't you? Get away from all these charts and lists. We can go by Parkview. I'll tell Malcolm about the seating change—he wants to talk to me about the ushers anyway—then we can take a drive in the countryside."

I had been hunched over the table, focused on wedding minutiae for hours. "Getting outside sounds wonderful." I left the wedding preparations spread across the table, and in a few minutes, we were cruising along a country lane. Tall hedgerows on either side of the road were dotted with the red berries, rose hips, and blackberries of autumn. Alex had lowered the top on his convertible MG Midget, and the brilliant September sun beat down on us while the wind whipped my hair over my eyes. I'd been surprised to see only one sticky note on the dash. It was held on with an extra layer of tape so that the wind didn't whisk it away. It fluttered back and forth in the breeze with the words "Parkview" and the date of our wedding, three weeks away.

At the gates of Parkview, we paused to speak to the man at the ticket kiosk, who waved us through when Alex said we were meeting Malcolm Stewart about wedding plans. We zipped down the oak-lined drive. The trees on either side were already showing hints of topaz in their leaves. Parkview, built with the local honey-colored limestone, came into view with its elegant architecture. A divided staircase rose to a portico with Corinthian columns. Two wings stretched out behind the central block of the house, creating a U-shape.

Alex parked in the area reserved for tourists, which was located behind a tall hedge that concealed the rows of cars and tour buses from the stately home. Parkview was on their summer season and was open every day. In a few weeks the schedule would shift to weekends only for the winter season.

The tourists followed the signs to the entrance, but Alex and I took a gravel path that ran along the west wing of the house. Beatrice and her staff worked in a suite of rooms at the end of the west wing. The estate office area was more low-key than the rest of the house—no heirloom furniture or priceless art—but it was still imposing. A chandelier glittered in the middle of the ornate plaster of the ceiling, and drapes, heavy with fringe, framed tall windows.

The oversized panel door at the end of the room, Beatrice's private office, was dark, which I knew meant she was probably overseeing some activity at Parkview or participating in a local village event. If she'd been here, Beatrice would have taken a few moments to speak to us. Desks with computers ranged around the room, but they were empty, except for one at the far end of the room, where Ella sat. Most of the guides and managers were out, escorting tourists and supervising the day-to-day activities of the house.

Ella was turned away from us, but I recognized her reddish-brown hair and slim figure. In her early twenties, Ella had been a waitress at one of the local pubs, then she'd taken a job working at Parkview as a maid during one of their re-creations of a Regency country house party, which was where I'd gotten to know her. It wasn't long after that weekend that Beatrice had hired her to work as a publicity assistant, along with the also newly hired publicity director, Malcolm. When I'd met her, Ella was set on getting out of Nether Woodsmoor and moving to London, but then she happily settled into the job at Parkview. I thought part of her new contentment with village life had to do with the fact that she enjoyed her job, but a certain young police constable was also part of the equation. Lucas Tally worked in the neighboring town of Hedgely, and I'd seen Ella and Lucas together several times in the pub and around the village.

Ella closed a file drawer and turned. I said hello, but a mechanical roar came from the back of the room, drowning out my words. I hadn't seen Malcolm in the little alcove, which contained a few cabinets, a small refrigerator, a hotplate, and a blender beside the sink. After a slight break in the noise, Malcolm, in his signature tweed jacket, pushed a button on the blender a few more times, causing the noise to pulse through the room. The racket continued for almost a minute. Ella rolled her eyes.

I settled for waving at Ella as I made my way through the desks toward her. When I reached her, Malcolm switched off the blender, but my ears rang with an echo of the noise in the sudden quiet.

I said hello, and Malcolm swiveled his upper torso around to us. "Oh, I didn't hear you come in, Kate. And, Alex, too."

Malcolm's sweater vest of the day had a green-and-gray pattern. He always wore a sweater vest under his tweed jacket. He was as tall as Alex, who was over six feet. But while Alex was lean with wide shoulders that narrowed to a flat stomach, Malcolm's paunch pressed against the wool of the vest. I wondered if the layers were because he was cold. Stately homes were not known for their toasty rooms. It was only September and the office had a distinct coolness to it. Ella informed me that if they had a big event Malcolm added a bow tie. I'd never seen him wear one, though, so she might be pulling my leg.

Alex said to Malcolm, "I got your message about the ushers. If you have a few minutes, we can talk about it and another issue that's come up."

"Of course. Always a delight to discuss the wedding with you." Malcolm's tone conveyed the opposite of his words, but he nodded, causing his fringe of pale brown hair that frizzed out around his ears to tremble. His hair was receding from his forehead, and in the time I'd known him, I'd noticed that as his hairline marched backward, he let the fringe of hair that remained grow longer. "Just let me finish this." He disconnected the blender and poured a slushy lime-green substance into a tall plastic glass. Malcolm raised the blender and looked back to us. "Would you like a smoothie? I have more than enough for everyone to have a sample. It's my own blend of kale, sweet grass, spinach, and fruit."

Behind his back, Ella mouthed the word, "No," with an emphatic shake of her head.

I stifled a grin. "No, thank you. Kind of you to offer." Malcolm's formal way of speaking always seemed to rub off on me. With his fussy adherence to tradition and his prim manners, I felt like I was dealing with someone from another era and was happy that Alex was along today and had promised to take the lead on the conversation about the seating chart.

"I make it a practice to never drink anything green," Alex said, and Malcolm inclined his head, silent disapproval in every line of his body. Malcolm plunged a straw into his concoction then gestured for Alex to take a seat at his desk. I dropped into a seat beside Ella's desk.

"So how's everything, wedding-wise?" she asked, her attention focused on a printout.

"Coming along. Why are you frowning so fiercely at that stack of papers?"

She quickly closed a file. A neon pink sticker with the words *Flower Arrangement Options* was stuck to the front. "Is it that noticeable?" Her gaze darted around the room's empty desks then settled briefly on Malcolm.

"Well, yes," I said. "You don't usually look so stressed. Is everything okay?" Ella had a cheerful personality, especially when it came to her work at Parkview.

"Everything is fine with the wedding." She scanned the room again, and for a second I thought she looked almost afraid, but then she smiled brightly. "It's nothing about that."

"Can't talk about it now?"

"No." Her phone buzzed with a message. "I have to go to the entry hall. The guests for Greenways Cottage have arrived, and I'm covering for Carl." She locked the file in a drawer.

"How is Carl?" I asked. Carl Buxby handled all of Parkview Hall's lodging from the guest rooms in the house, which were available to book for overnight stays, to the holiday cottages that were scattered around the estate grounds and the village. "I heard he's in the hospital." Louise, my friend and the owner of the White Duck pub, heard all the gossip around Nether Woodsmoor. She said Carl had passed out last week. The staff at Parkview couldn't bring him around, so they called for an ambulance. I looked toward Carl's desk, which was covered in its usual mass of binders, printed pages, and magazines. An assortment of pens, paperclips, and "while you were out" messages were scattered across the stacks. It surprised me that Carl, who always looked immaculate in person, thrived in such a disorganized work area.

"Doing much better now that they've sorted out that he fainted because he has an irregular heartbeat."

"That sounds bad. He seems so healthy. It's hard to imagine him in the hospital." As far as I could tell, Carl spent all his leisure time on the numerous bike trails that wound through the countryside. I often caught sight of him on the path behind my cottage, his aerodynamic helmet nearly touching his forearms as he hunched over his bike. Village gossip was that he was in his mid-forties and had moved to Nether Woodsmoor after a divorce.

"Apparently he'll be fine as long as he takes his medicine. He should be back at work in a few days." She closed a window on her computer then pushed in her desk chair. "I'm sorry I can't stay."

"No, go. Do what you need to." I heard the words ". . .that will never do," from Malcolm. I said to Ella, "Time for me to weigh in with Malcolm, I think."

I shifted to sit in the other open chair in front of Malcolm's desk as Alex said, "I don't see why there's an issue. It's what Kate and I want."

"It's not appropriate." Malcolm pinched his lips. Since the glass with his green smoothie filled to the brim still sat on the corner of his desk, I assumed the subject of open seating caused his sour look, not his drink. He steepled his fingers and leaned toward us, his tone similar to what one would use with school-children who don't understand the value of learning their times tables. "You see, one of the reasons people choose to be married at Parkview is the sense of tradition and pageantry. A certain formality is expected." He reached for the handle of a file drawer. "In fact, according to the event contract—"

"We don't need to see the contract. I'm sure it is one of the things covered, but I'm equally sure that Beatrice would not mind if we did things a little differently. Blame it on us being Americans, if you like." Alex smiled as he said the last words, but his tone held an unyielding quality—a rare thing for Alex—that caused me to look at him out of the corner of my eye.

Malcolm's lips squeezed tighter. I imagined Alex's use of "Beatrice" instead of her formal title "Lady Stone" is what deep-ened the disapproving look on his face. I'd only heard him refer to Beatrice by her title, even though she asked everyone to call her by her first name. "I don't think Lady Stone would approve of that sort of change."

Alex's smile became fixed, and I realized he was angry, a state so rare with him that I jumped in quickly. "Really? You don't think she'd like it? Because I think she wouldn't care at all. In fact, let's give her a call." I took out my cell phone. Her number was in my contact list because when we had filmed at Parkview I had to call her frequently. I didn't feel the least bit intimidated about dialing her number.

Malcolm shifted his chair forward with a jerk, and I thought he was about to reach for my phone, but he restrained himself. "I'm sure that won't be necessary," he said before I could select her name. He smoothed his hand over his flyaway hair, which was standing out around his ears.

"Excellent." I dropped my phone into my jacket pocket.

Malcolm patted a stack of papers into alignment. "Since you're so set on it...I suppose we could make an exception, this once."

After we left the business office, Alex didn't speak until we were halfway down the drive. "Officious little twit."

I held my hair back from my face as the wind tried to tease it out of my hand. "I agree, but apparently he's a good event coordinator. And it's settled. We got what we wanted. That's the main thing."

We passed through the open gates at the entrance, then Alex merged onto the road. "That's true." His hand relaxed on the steering wheel as he followed the curve of the road. He shook his head. "I can see how this wedding stuff can stress you out."

"I feel a little better. If one conversation with Malcolm can put you on edge, then I don't feel so bad for being annoyed with him so much. Where are we going? That was the turn for the village."

"It's a surprise," Alex said.

CHAPTER 2

"$\mathscr{A}$nd that's all I'm telling you about it. No hints," Alex said as we drove along the lane. "So, new topic. I got an email from my dad today. He's arriving the day before the wedding."

"That's cutting it close, isn't it? Since he's coming from Chile won't he need to adjust to the time zone here?" Alex's dad worked in the diplomatic corps and was currently assigned to the U.S. Embassy in Chile. Alex was American, but had grown up moving around the world, following his dad from one government post to the next.

"No, he'll be fine. He's used to international travel. He'll sleep on the plane." I felt Alex look at me out of the corner of his eye. "Any change in plans from your dad?"

"No." I sighed. "Still not coming."

Alex reached across the gearshift for my hand. "I'm sorry. I thought he might change his mind if you called."

I lifted one shoulder. "He's not like your dad. He hates to fly. Not in an I-don't-like-it way. It's true anxiety." I looked at the trees, their gold and brown leaves flashing in the wind. "I didn't really expect him to come."

Since my parents' divorce a few years ago, I hadn't seen much of my dad. His parenting style had always been of the *laissez-faire* type. He was content to let me range where I wanted in my friendships, hobbies, and reading—especially my reading. He'd always had a love for books and encouraged me to read widely. His attitude was quite a contrast to my mother's helicopter-style parenting. His abrupt announcement that he wanted a divorce and he was leaving his management job to buy out an independent bookstore owner in Kansas City had been a shock on one level—I guess you never expect your parents to get divorced—but on another level I wasn't completely surprised. I'd known my mom and dad were intensely unhappy.

Alex said, "Maybe I shouldn't have encouraged you to phone him."

I shifted in the seat, angling toward Alex. "Don't think that. It was a good thing. I want to stay in touch with him more. I *was* upset with him after the divorce, but that's in the past. We've worked it out. He came out to see me in California when Mom went off the rails, and we patched things up."

Alex said, "Well, it does sound as if he left you holding the bag, so to speak. With your mom, I mean."

It was true. Dad exiting our life as casually as though he were checking out of a hotel room had thrown my mom into a tailspin. Not having the most stable of personalities, Mom had leaned a little too heavily on prescription medication, so I left graduate school and moved home. Thankfully, after counseling and rehab, she'd regained her equilibrium. I'd been able to take the location scouting job in England without worrying about her constantly. "I did resent my dad for a while, but now—" I shook my head. "I couldn't stay mad at him. He did what he did, and that's that. All those things—that chain of events— brought me here. If I'd finished grad school, I probably wouldn't have moved to Nether Woodsmoor and met you."

Alex looked away from the road and smiled at me, and I felt a fluttery sensation in my stomach that had nothing to do with the abrupt dip and twist in the road.

"That's very adult of you. Was your dad's answer a flat no?" Alex asked. "When you called and asked him to come to the wedding, I mean?"

"No, he sounded...regretful. I think he would like to be here."

"Then how does he feel about boats?" Alex watched the road as it curved through a belt of trees.

"I don't think he has strong feelings about boats. What are you thinking? A cruise ship?"

"Why not? There's still time. He can get from New York to London in six or seven days. If he can be away from the store that long."

"I hadn't thought of a cruise."

"My mom does it all the time. She's extremely fond of cruise ships. She likes them almost as much as high-end hotel rooms on the Riviera—French or Italian Riviera, doesn't matter which, as long as it's part of the Riviera. Or she'll take the Caribbean in a pinch. But back to your dad. He could be here in a week or so without going through airport security or breaking ten thousand feet."

"I'll mention it to him. Maybe send him an email or something."

"Tell him to call me if he wants details on any of the ships. I can ask my mom for a recommendation. She'll know which deck, even which cabins, to pick."

"What about your mom? When does she arrive?"

"She's in London that week. She'll come up for the day of the wedding then take the train back to London that night."

"She's not even staying one night?" I asked.

"It will work out perfectly. A few hours is the maximum amount of time she needs to exercise her maternal inclinations. Then she can get back to shopping and lunching and tanning."

Alex glanced at me. "Sounds shallow, I know, but I'm not exaggerating."

I hadn't met Alex's parents yet. A trip to Chile wasn't exactly easy to work into our schedule when we were starting a business and planning a wedding—not to mention the expense of two tickets to South America. But his mom seemed to spend most of her time in European resorts, which were much closer. However, the few times Alex had floated the suggestion that the three of us meet before the wedding, his mom always replied, "Sounds lovely, but it's not possible at the moment...perhaps later."

Alex's parents were also divorced, but his mom was the one who left. Alex didn't talk about his mom often, and when he did, she was one of the few subjects that caused his easy-going nature to disappear. Her flighty disposition was the reason Alex was so involved in his younger sister's life. With his dad constantly posted around the world, Alex gave Grace's life the stability that a thirteen-year-old needed. The close location of her school to Nether Woodsmoor was one reason Alex lived in the village. Grace could come "home" to his cottage during school holidays.

"Your mom doesn't want to spend some time with Grace?" I asked.

"No, she does not. Speaking of Grace, she says she has the perfect thing for your 'something blue,' but wouldn't tell me what it is. I told her you might already have something picked out for that. I'd suggest you get something quick, if you don't have something already."

"I'm sure it will be fine."

"You've obviously not been on the receiving end of gifts from a thirteen-year-old girl. I have an extensive collection of lumpy winter scarves that you are free to borrow anytime. One is red with orange stripes, and another has purple dots on baby blue."

"That's where those came from?" I'd wondered about his taste in winter scarves, which didn't go with his usual casual style of a solid-colored shirt, jeans, and his broken-in leather jacket.

"You've been warned." Alex eased off the gas, his gaze on the trees on the side of the road. "Watch out, or you might end up with some sort of itchy blue scarf wrapped around your neck when you walk down the aisle. She's thrilled you asked her to be in the wedding. She mentions it every time I talk to her."

Alex and I had decided to go with a small wedding party—extremely small. He had asked Brent, one of his oldest friends, to be his best man, and I asked my friend Melissa to be my maid of honor. Grace, as a junior bridesmaid, completed the group.

"I'm glad she wants to be a part of it." When Grace had learned Alex and I were dating, she wasn't happy about it. I was extremely glad she'd come around to the idea of us as a couple.

"Here it is." Alex turned the car onto a road that cut in between a gap in the trees, then slowed as we traveled down the narrow lane. Oaks tinged with autumn colors crowded against both sides of the strip of asphalt. We emerged into a clearing where a cottage of honey-colored stone glowed in the sun. Ivy softened the flat facade of the building, tracing across the stone, then around the window, and finally reaching to the steep roof. The dark leaves of the ivy bobbed in the breeze. Alex stopped the car in front of the white door.

"What is this place? I've never seen it." We couldn't be more than a few miles from Nether Woodsmoor. "I thought I knew all homes and estates around here."

"This was a storage building, for carts, I believe. Part of Parkview's extensive stables and outbuildings. Until about nine months ago it was boarded up and vacant, but then Beatrice decided to 'freshen it up,' she said. She's calling it Cart Cottage."

To stay ahead of Parkview's astronomical upkeep, Beatrice had renovated several cottages on the grounds and some in Nether Woodsmoor to attract people on holiday. Charging admission to tour Parkview and hosting events like weddings were other streams of income for the stately home. "Quaint and cozy. I doubt they'll have trouble booking it."

Alex said, "I was thinking it would be a good place to spend the first part of our honeymoon."

"Oh, Alex, I love that idea." Our honeymoon, a three-day trip to Venice, was a gift from Alex's dad, but the departure dates hadn't lined up exactly with the wedding date, and our flight wasn't scheduled to depart until several days after the ceremony. Movers were arriving the day after the wedding to shift my things to Alex's cottage. Ivy Cottage was bigger and would be perfect after we returned from our honeymoon, but we wouldn't be able to stay there immediately after the ceremony. Before the honeymoon plans had been booked, Beatrice had scheduled workmen to repair several cracks in the cottage's stone walls, thinking it would be the ideal time for the work to be done since we'd be out of town. The repair work did need to be done, so Alex and I had decided we'd spend the days between the wedding and the departure for the honeymoon in a bed and breakfast or a hotel.

"No, wait, don't decide yet," Alex said. "You haven't seen the inside." I followed him to the front door where he worked an oversized antique key out of his pocket. "No room service, no spa, no minibar." He fit the key into the lock. "We could have that if we stayed in a posh hotel."

He pushed open the door and waved me inside. Beatrice must have had some walls knocked down because the whole downstairs was one open room. On the left was a kitchen with a two-burner cooktop, a microwave, and mini-fridge. A round wooden table and two chairs were positioned in front of a large window at the back of the room overlooking a view of a meadow. Dry-stone walls crisscrossed the green hills rolling away into the distance. On the right side of the room, a large sofa covered in cheerful stripes sat in front of a fireplace. Shelf-lined walls on either side of the fireplace were bursting with books. Thick wooden beams ran overhead. In the back corner of the room, a circular iron staircase twisted upward.

I turned to Alex. "Who needs room service?"

~

Three days until the wedding

"...and I *must* get a hat." My mom hitched her carry-on bag higher on her shoulder. "You'll have to take me shopping. I couldn't find anything in California. Nothing appropriate *at all*. Only straw beachy things. Well, that's not quite true. I did see a horrible creation dripping with feathers and beads in black. Can you believe it? Black! I told the salesgirl—they're all so young now and know absolutely *nothing* about looking elegant—I told her it was not at all what I need for a wedding at an English country manor."

Mom paused for a breath, and I said, "Your hair. You stopped coloring it." We were standing in the airport terminal and those were the first words I'd managed to say since she came through the doors from baggage claim. I was surprised to see the streak of white that ran from the center of my mom's forehead and down the left side of her chin-length bob. I couldn't remember a time when she hadn't dyed the white section to match the rest of her chestnut brown hair. The shock of white hair is a hereditary condition, and my mom used to check my hair when I was little to see if I would have it as well. She was relieved when my hair remained a solid mahogany brown. As a little kid, I had picked up on her dislike of her own streak of white and thought it was a bad thing. When I hit my teenage years, though, I thought a white streak in my hair would have been cool.

"I decided it was time to show it off." She shook her hair off her face in an imitation of a shampoo commercial. Then she leaned close, her bravado dropping away. "What do you think? Good choice?"

"Great choice." I was glad to see her embracing something that she'd always felt self-conscious about. "It looks good on you. Come on, the car is this way. I had to park a long way from the terminal—" I broke off as my mom retreated a few steps and retrieved a luggage cart. "Is that all yours?"

"Of course. Why would I push around someone else's luggage?"

I picked up the umbrella that rested on top of the suitcases. It was about three feet long and had a curved wooden handle on one end and a sharp silver tip on the other. "This looks dangerous. I'm surprised they let you through security with it."

"Kate, it's *England*. Everyone needs an umbrella at all times. Look, it opens automatically."

She took it from me, touched a button, and the black canopy bloomed into fullness, cutting off my view of most of the terminal. I put my finger on the silver tip and pushed the thing out of my face. "Impressive, but it's not raining today."

"It will be," Mom said confidently. "It *always* rains in England. All the guidebooks say so." She hit the button again and the canopy retracted as quickly as it had expanded.

"That is cool," I said, impressed. I'd lived in England for a year and didn't have an auto-retracting umbrella.

"Wait until you see my money belt." She patted the bulge at her waist. "It's got layers to protect from electronic pickpocketing—can you imagine? I can get everything in it—my credit cards, passport, and phone *and* it's so slender it's practically invisible. Next to an umbrella, a money belt is the most important thing to have when you travel."

It sounded like she was quoting from a guidebook so I said, "Sounds great. You wait here, and I'll bring the car around." I eyed the load of suitcases nearly toppling off the cart. "I might have to make two trips to Nether Woodsmoor."

"Whatever for?"

"One with your luggage, then one with you. I brought Alex's

car. You said you packed light so I thought..." I should have known better than to take my mother at her word.

"Oh, don't be silly, Kate. I'm sure it will fit. It all went in the airport shuttle fine."

"But I don't drive a van," I said. "Oh, and you don't have to wear a hat to the wedding," I added as I maneuvered the cart through clusters of travelers.

"Not have a hat?" Several people looked toward us as Mom's voice bounced across the hard surfaces of the airport. "*Of course* I'll wear a hat. It's an English wedding."

"You sound like Malcolm," I muttered and wedged the cart through the exit door. Louder, I said, "I asked my friend Louise— she lives here, you know, and she's been to several weddings. She said hats are optional."

"Optional." Mom gave a little laugh that conveyed how out of the loop I was. "It's *mandatory*, dear. I looked it up on the Internet."

I decided to abandon the argument. Some discussions with my mother were like that—discretion being the better part of valor. "You wait here with your luggage. I'll get as close as I can with the car."

~

Two hours later, I pulled into the airport for the second time that day. I'd been lucky to get her large suitcases in Alex's MG *without* my mom. I thought I could squeeze in the last two smaller bags for the return trip to Nether Woodsmoor—as long as my mom held one on her lap. I parked, hiked to the terminal, and headed for the little coffee shop located outside the security checkpoint where my mom said she'd wait for me.

The bright white streak in her hair made her easy to find. She was perched at a minuscule table, an empty cup and a plate of crumbs in front of her. She was turned partially away from me as she said something to a slight young man seated at the next table. He had a beard and one of those haircuts that are shaved on the sides and long on top. He leaned forward and touched his table as he emphasized his points. The long swath of hair fell forward over one eye. He brushed it back and continued talking and pressing the table. My mom seemed to disagree because she shook her head.

She glanced my way. As soon as she saw me, she shoved back her chair, threw the strap of her carry-on bag on her shoulder, and grabbed the handle of her rolling suitcase. She seized the umbrella from the back of her chair then motored over to meet me outside the area where the tables were grouped. "There you are! I'm practically asleep on my feet."

"It looked like you were in an intense discussion." I transferred her carry-on tote to my shoulder and reached for her rolling suitcase.

"What? A discussion? No, I wasn't talking to anyone."

"You weren't talking to him? That young guy over there waving to you?"

"What?" She narrowed her eyes as she looked over her shoulder then jerked back toward me. She grabbed the handle of the rolling suitcase out of my hand. "Oh…I think he was…on the same flight. He wanted to know…where to exchange his dollars for pounds."

"There's a currency exchange right around the corner—ouch! That's my foot."

"Oops. Sorry, dear." Mom angled the suitcase away from my toes but didn't stop moving in the direction of the exit. "I told him I had no idea where it was. I'm sure he can read the signs for himself," she said over her shoulder.

I wiggled my toes, glad I had worn loafers, and glanced at the man. He was lounging back in the chair, one foot propped up on a beat-up suitcase, his attention now focused on the screen of his phone.

I knew that breezy artificial tone that Mom had used. I'd heard it when I was a kid when she stuffed her purchases from her secret shopping sprees in the back of the closet. I could hear her voice as she closed the closet door. "Just doing a bit of tidying up. No, no need to help me. I'll finish up later." And I couldn't count the times she'd used that tone when she asked me to her condo for "a bite of dinner" that turned out to be an ambush blind date with some guy that she thought would be perfect for me. It hadn't taken me long to learn to vet all her dinner invitations.

I watched the guy for a moment. Mom wasn't still matchmaking, was she? No, that would be crazy, especially if she thought that skinny guy with his hipster hair could even compare with Alex. I turned and hurried after her, catching up to her outside the main doors. She stood on the edge of the sidewalk, scanning the parking lot. "Mom, what is going on?"

She raised her eyebrows, her expression as innocent as a saint in a medieval painting. "What are you talking about?"

"Never mind. The car's this way." I knew from long experience that when she opened her eyes wide and put on that guileless expression, I wouldn't get anything else out of her. The subject was closed as far as she was concerned, but something was up. She was either scheming or covering up something.

"Here we are." I unlocked the doors of the MG the old-fashioned way, by inserting the key into the lock and twisting. The MG was an antique and didn't have power anything.

My mom stood immobile a few feet behind me. "But that's not a car. That's a...toy." She took a few steps to the side and examined it from another angle. "Was this some sort of clown car? Why are you laughing? You have to admit it does look like something out of a circus."

"It's a real car—a classic. You act like you've never seen a small car before."

24

"We have lots of small cars in California, but not like *this*. I bet it's barely bigger than your Uncle Ed's golf cart."

Once we were on the way back to Nether Woodsmoor I said, "I don't know what was going on back there at the coffee shop, but if you think that guy you were talking to is any match for Alex, you're crazy. If you think I can do better, and you're set on making trouble for Alex and me, you should reconsider. Alex is kind and thoughtful. He's funny and smart. We laugh at the same things. He loves me—which I still find amazing because he knows me really well now—and I love him. We're getting married next week."

"Inside voice, Kate, please. No need to shout, especially in such a small space." Mom shifted the carry-on bag in her lap a little, and I felt her steady gaze on me. "I think Alex is wonderful. I'm happy for you."

"Are you? You have no secret plans to…I don't know…change things?" I couldn't bring myself to say the word *sabotage*.

"No! I'd never do something like that. I'm thrilled for you—for both of you. You have no idea what a *relief* it is to me to know you'll be settled in a good marriage. You've no *idea* how much I worried about you. But now that you've got Alex, I can do other things—move on."

The urban landscape of the city had fallen away, and we entered the wide stretch of countryside with its patchwork green hills splashed here and there with swaths of gold, bronze, and deep red. I kept my eyes on the road. My marital status had been a sort of hobby for my mom. She'd always been focused on finding me a husband and getting me settled. I'd worried that after I was actually married she might find the transition difficult. But as I glanced at her now I decided I couldn't have been more wrong. She looked happy and content and, yes, excited for me. "You mean the genealogy project?" I asked.

"It's so fascinating. I can't wait to tell you about our English ancestors. Did you know we're related to a woman who helped the police solve a murder in the twenties? They called her the high society detective. While I'm here I want to run up to London and see the house she lived in. It's a museum now. And then there's that singer, Tom Davis. He might be a cousin! A distant one and by marriage of course, but *still*. It's so exciting to think of it. If his wife had a brother named Lucas whose mother was married to Ronald Westings, then he *is* related."

"And Ronald Westings is…?"

"Grandfather Gavin's uncle," she said in a tone that indicated everyone knew that. "I will say this for your father—he may not have been good for much, but he does have some excellent relatives. Imagine being related to Tom Davis!" My face must have looked blank because she added, "That eighties group—oh, what was their name? I loved their music. Something about zeros on their side…"

"The Edge of Zero? That group? They're one of those one-hit wonders, right?"

"No, they had plenty of hits…well, several from the same album."

"So, they were a one-hit-album wonder."

"Do you know any of their songs?"

"Before my time, Mom." I'd heard of the group and remembered running across one of those pop culture biography shows about them once when I was searching for something to watch. If I was pressed into a trivia game at the pub, I might be able to come up with a few of their song titles, but my mom was clearly more enchanted with the idea of being related to these people than I was.

"I can tell you're not interested," she said, "but *I* think it's thrilling that we're related to these people who have done unique things. There's a good chance we're related to that explorer who went to the north pole, too. That would be through your Aunt Millie. I'm still tracking that one down."

"That's great." I was glad she had an interest besides marrying me off.

"I've also taken up bridge."

"Bridge?"

"I know. Can you believe it? Me! I always thought I was such a dunce, but I'm actually good at it. Shocking, I know, but there it is."

"That's great," I said again, then added, "But if you're not still recruiting suitors for me, then what was going on with the man at the coffee shop?"

She became interested in the stitching on the bag in her lap. "He was on my flight, and he was chatting about some things. Rather pushy. I can't stand people like that. I just wanted to get away, that's all. Oh, look—sheep."

CHAPTER 3

ONE DAY BEFORE THE WEDDING

*M*elissa said something, but since she was speaking around several straight pins held between her teeth, I couldn't understand her. I assumed she wanted me to turn. I rotated a quarter turn, which must have been the correct thing to do because she nodded in satisfaction as she studied the hem of my wedding dress. She made the same noise again. I moved another quarter turn. I stood on a chair that we had placed in the center of my cottage's small front room. My head nearly brushed the heavy beams that lined the ceiling, but Melissa had insisted she needed to see the hem at eye level to make sure it was exactly right.

Melissa was a friend from the documentary crew. She'd worked in Costume and had helped me find my wedding gown. When she'd offered to go shopping with me, I'd been thrilled. Having a professional give me advice seemed like a great idea, but then I'd had second thoughts. Melissa's personal style was eclectic and wide-ranging. She loved to wear different looks and experiment with unusual styles, so I wasn't sure what she'd recommend. But she'd spotted the perfect gown for me. She'd pulled a vintage gown off the rack at a second-hand shop and said, "Classic and elegant. You'd better try this one on. It's very you."

Melissa mumbled, and I turned again. I ran my hand over the fitted bodice that flared to a gentle swell of fabric that floated around my feet. The ivory dress had a lace overlay that created an off-the-shoulder neckline, which ran straight across my shoulders to form cap sleeves. "It's hard to believe that I'm getting married tomorrow." All the planning and coordination, all the build-up—everything would come together tomorrow. At least, I hoped it would. I'd been through my mental checklists many times, and I felt like I'd been on the phone with Malcolm more than I had with Alex during the last few days. My cottage had been furnished when I moved in, so I only had my clothes and personal things to move to Alex's cottage. Everything was packed and ready for the movers, except my suitcase, which was going with me to Parkview tonight. Parkview was now closed for weekday tours, but it remained open to the public on weekends. This week and next, the stately home's guest rooms were completely filled with our wedding guests.

Melissa gave the hem a final tweak. "You say that like there was any doubt. I knew from the first time I saw you and Alex together that you'd walk down the aisle. Took *you* a bit longer to get to this point than I thought it would, though."

"You're one to talk. I'm getting to the altar faster than you and Paul."

She focused on putting away all the pins. "Yeah. Well, we'll see."

She leaned back on her heels, and her cowboy boots creaked with the movement. She wore fitted jeans and a shirt of her own design that blended the fringe of a western look with a flowing poet-style shirt. It sounded like something that wouldn't look good together, but Melissa made it interesting and fun. Tomorrow she'd be in a demure gown of pale pink as my maid of honor. She'd picked it out and assured me that it was perfect for the wedding and that she'd love wearing it. "I'll channel my inner Duchess Kate," she'd said. "It's your wedding, and you're all about classic styles."

She surveyed me from head to toe. "I think you're ready."

"I doubt that."

"Okay, sartorially prepared. How about that?"

"That, I agree with. You've been a huge help."

"All in a day's work."

As she packed away her scissors then checked the floor for stray pins, a knock sounded on the back door, then a voice called out, "Kate, it's me, Grace."

"Come in." I stepped down from the chair and heard the jingle of a dog collar, which meant that Grace had brought Alex's greyhound, Slink, along with her. Grace had arrived from school yesterday. She had already been fitted in her blush-colored junior bridesmaid dress, which was now hanging on her door in Ivy Cottage.

Slink trotted into the room and went straight for Melissa, who was still on the floor. I sidestepped Slink's tail, which was whipping back and forth in excitement as she planted a lick on Melissa's face. "Gross." Melissa wiped her cheek, but she petted Slink's narrow head as she said to her, "You know I'm a cat person, right?"

Grace rounded the corner and stopped. "Kate, you look absolutely smashing!"

"Thanks." Grace was as American as Alex, but she'd picked up many expressions from her British classmates. Yesterday she'd been "knackered" when she arrived from the bus ride. I still couldn't get over how much taller and more grown-up she looked. In the last few months, she'd grown into a young woman instead of a gangly pre-teen. She'd changed out of her school uniform as soon as she arrived in the village, and now wore a pair of skinny jeans with a lime green long-sleeved T-shirt that complemented her dark hair and eyes.

Melissa gave Slink a final pat on the head then pointed a finger at her. "No slobbering or shedding on the dress." Slink opened her mouth and panted happily back at her. Melissa said to me, "I have to go and change. Paul's picking me up for the not-a-rehearsal dinner at the pub." She picked up her sewing kit and waved as she headed for the door.

I'd learned that in the UK wedding rehearsals and rehearsal dinners were not usually part of wedding traditions. Malcolm had been scandalized when I'd asked what time we'd hold the rehearsal. "We don't need a rehearsal," he'd said. "Everything will go flawlessly. We often have three weddings a week," he'd added when I'd been about to protest.

I'd let the wedding rehearsal go—how hard could it be to walk down the aisle? But I felt a flutter of nerves. Steps, I reminded myself. It's one foot in front of the other. No big deal. *With lots of people watching you*, my nerves whispered. I pushed away those worries and focused on tonight at the pub. I could worry about tripping tomorrow. Tonight, Alex's dad was hosting an evening at the pub in place of a rehearsal dinner.

"That's why I'm here," Grace said. "Alex wants to know if you're ready to go."

I closed the front door behind Melissa and looked down at my dress. "Not quite. You can go on, and I'll meet you there in a few minutes."

"Okay," she said but made no move to leave.

I paused with my hand on the stair's bannister. "Do you want to wait for me?"

"Ah—no. I wanted to show you this." She pulled a small jeweler's box out of the back pocket of her jeans and flicked it open. An opal necklace rested against the pale blue satin. "I thought you might like to wear this for your something blue?"

"That's gorgeous—and that's so nice of you to think of me. You didn't buy that, did you?" I knew she got an allowance from her dad, and while there weren't many opportunities to purchase things while at school, I certainly didn't want her spending her money on me.

"It was my grandmother's. It's part of a set with earrings. Alex said I can only wear it on special occasions. I thought maybe you might like to wear the necklace, and I could, maybe, wear the earrings. Share the set—like sisters share things, you know." She hurried on before I could answer and added, "I know it's mostly white, but it does have some blue in it...it sort of sparkles blue."

"I'd love to wear it, Grace. It's perfect."

~

After Grace left, I tucked the jewelry box with the necklace into my suitcase, touched that she wanted to share the set with me. I zipped the suitcase closed and set it aside. Tonight I would be at Parkview in the rose room. Most of the wedding party were staying in the stately home. My mom had been ensconced in the green room since she arrived, and Alex's dad was staying there, too.

I slipped out of my dress, glad that it had a side zipper, and hung it up with all the care that Melissa would have lavished on a period gown. I changed into a V-neck sweater, khaki pants, and high-heeled boots, then hurried back downstairs.

I slipped on my jacket as I stepped out the front door and locked it. I turned and stopped dead on the top step of the little porch that fronted the cottage as I stared at the man with longish gray hair and glasses who stood hesitating at my front gate.

"Dad," I said after a moment and trotted down the steps. I opened the gate and stepped into his hug. I normally like my personal space, but I squeezed tight against his shoulder. "You came." The familiar waft of his citrus aftershave combined with the faint but distinctive chemical smell of a dry-cleaned jacket took me back to my childhood. I was six years old and at the breakfast table as Dad gave me a quick hug before he left for work. I pulled away, almost expecting him to say, "Learn something interesting at school today, kiddo."

When I looked at his face, I was struck by the new lines that traced along his forehead. Grooves that I didn't remember on either side of his mouth deepened as he smiled at me. "Look at you. So beautiful. So grown-up."

"What are you doing here?" He flinched slightly at my words, and I squeezed his arm. "Not that I'm not glad to see you. I'm thrilled you're here. Thrilled! I'm a little—shocked, too, I guess. I was so sure you wouldn't be here." My vision had gone blurry. I blinked quickly, realizing that I hadn't even admitted to myself how much I wanted my whole family to be at the wedding.

"It's your wedding. I couldn't miss it." He looked a little misty-eyed, too, and cleared his throat. "Although, I would have appreciated a State-side wedding. Plenty of nice places over there, you know. That way I wouldn't have had a woman tell me about her fourteen grandchildren—with pictures—for eight hours."

"You flew?"

"Had too," he said. "I left it too late to do anything else."

"I'm—I actually don't know what to say. Wait, yes, I do. Grace would say 'gobsmacked' and that's it, exactly. I'm gobsmacked. Thank you for coming. I know how hard that must have been for you."

He looked away and focused on the gate. "I've messed up... well...many things. Too many to count, you know." He transferred his gaze to me. "I didn't want to add anything else to the list."

I smiled at him, understanding what he was trying to say about the past. "I'm glad you're here. I'd love for you to come in, but we're having a little get-together at the pub tonight." I motioned to the lane and the village. "It starts in a few minutes. Will you come with me?"

"I don't want to be in the way."

"You won't be. We have to catch up. You can meet Alex…and everyone else."

"All right, I can try a pint of the local brew." He fell into step beside me. "Alex seems like a fine one."

I stopped. "You've already met him? When did you get here?"

"I arrived yesterday. I've been at the inn, sleeping off the time change."

"But you can't stay there. I have a room reserved for you at Parkview. I thought—I hoped—that you'd come. You can move up there tonight," I said quickly in a matter-of-fact voice because he was blinking again.

"Yes. Good idea."

"Now, *have* you met Alex?" I asked as we resumed walking.

"Only on the phone. And I think he's definitely right about a cruise—that's how I'm going home."

The pub was not far. My dad was in the middle of telling me how ridiculous he found airport screening practices when we arrived at the pub, and a rusty mint-green Range Rover pulled up beside us. It belonged to Parkview and was used to ferry guests to and from the village. Alex's dad, Randall, a distinguished man with dark hair and a touch of gray at his temples, dressed in an immaculate charcoal suit, climbed out. I'd met him yesterday and moved to say hello to him and begin the introductions, but he turned and helped my mom out of the car. I was surprised to see she was wearing a tailored black sheath. The plain lines of the dress seemed a little unlike her usual style, but then she reached in the car and picked up a fringed shawl in a bright red-and-gold pattern. She tossed it around her shoulders, hooked her umbrella over her arm, and reached for Randall's arm. My mom was not one to overlook a handsome escort.

Dad hadn't noticed them. "...pulled every third person for inspection," he was saying. "Like back in grade school when we had to number off. How they think a terrorist couldn't figure out the pattern and move to a different place in line, I don't know..." His gaze connected with my mother's. The smile she'd tossed at Randall vanished.

Randall, like the excellent diplomat he was, recognized a delicate situation and melted away after greeting us and saying that he would see everyone inside.

My mother opened her mouth to say something, but I could tell from her expression that it wouldn't get us off on the right foot, so I said quickly, "Isn't it great that Dad could make it? I'm so glad my whole family is here."

She finally looked away from Dad to me. "Quite a surprise." My face must have shown how tense I was because she lowered her tone from freezing to merely chilly as she turned back to Dad. "Oliver. It's...good...to see you again." She sounded anything but pleased.

"You too, Ava." He reached out to shake her hand. "You look lovely."

My dad might have dropped everything and fled from our life in California, but he did have his moments.

I could see his words thawed her a bit more. "Thank you." She shook his hand.

I breathed a sigh of relief. "Let's go in." I was eager to get them into the pub and separated. I saw several friends once we were inside. Melissa and Paul were huddled together at one of the tall tables, and Louise whipped by, tray in hand. I was surprised to see Malcolm at the bar. I'd invited everyone in Parkview's estate office, but hadn't expected Malcolm to come. I passed Carl, who was circulating through the pub, looking dapper as usual. Today he sported a blue ascot with his open-collared shirt and jacket.

"Good to see you're feeling better," I said since I'd missed him every time I was in the estate office at Parkview lately. I was glad to see his color was good, and he looked as healthy as he always did.

He patted his chest. "Back to normal now." He leaned closer and said, "But don't tell Louise. She's still plying me with food and drink, and I like it."

I had a feeling it was more than sympathy that had Louise attending to Carl. He might have salt-and-pepper hair, but he was one of the few bachelors in Nether Woodsmoor under sixty. He lifted his drink. "Cheers."

"There's Alex and his dad," I said to my parents as they followed me through the crowd. Full introductions were performed, and Randall offered to get my dad a drink. My mom said she wanted to check her lipstick, so I pointed her in the direction of the loo, which left Alex and me alone for a few moments. I pulled him a few paces away from the crowd to a table in the corner. "You called my dad."

"Guilty."

He looked worried, so I said, "I'm so glad you did. How did you convince him to come?"

"I told him you wanted him here."

I frowned. "But I told him that."

"Yes, but sometimes when it comes from someone else the argument is more effective."

"Well, I'm glad he's here. At least, I think I'm glad. It was touch-and-go outside when he and my mom met face-to-face. It's not outright war between them, thank goodness, like it was years ago. They've declared a cease-fire—for now."

"Hmm. Well, we don't have to worry about my parents fighting. They never speak to each other." He reached for my hand. "Brent just got here. I want you to meet him. No stressful undercurrents there."

We made our way through the crowd to Alex's best man.

Brent was a short man in his late twenties with thick golden hair cut short around his ears and combed to the side in a retro *Mad Men* look. He and Alex did a quick guy hug with sharp smacks on the back, then Alex introduced me. Alex and Brent had been at several of the same diplomatic postings during the years they were growing up.

Brent twitched his tie straight and transferred his glass to his left hand. "Wonderful to meet you, Kate. You're more beautiful than Alex said."

"Thank you." I sent Alex a quick glance. "That's a lovely thing to say, but I'm sure you and Alex have better things to talk about besides what I look like."

"Busted," said Alex to Brent. "I told you she would see right through that fake embassy chit-chat."

Brent swirled the stir stick in his drink as he laughed. "Occupational hazard." Brent was in the foreign service and currently worked in the same embassy as Alex's dad.

"You do it very well, though." I hoped I hadn't gotten off on the wrong foot with Alex's best friend. "Small talk is not my thing —as you can tell."

Brent was the closest thing Alex had to a childhood friend, but looking at them side by side, I wouldn't have thought they had anything in common. Alex was in what he considered dressy clothes, a blue oxford shirt with an open collar and a pair of dark jeans, while Brent wore a dark suit and tie. Alex dressed down as a rule. He'd agreed to make an exception for the wedding and wear a tux. Alex was tall and lanky and had a relaxed, casual air about him while a sense of hyped up energy emanated from Brent. He was constantly moving, stepping forward or backward, smoothing down his tie, or swirling the stir stick in his drink.

"Then you and I must talk later." He leaned toward me as if he were about to confide in me. "I have plenty of stories to tell you about Alex."

"Save them for the reception," Alex said.

I heard something and looked at Alex. "Was that a shout?" The pub was crowded and the noise level was high, but I'd heard a sharp exclamation. It had sounded far away. "Maybe outside?"

"I didn't hear anything—" A screeching sound filled the air briefly, then cut off.

A murmur rippled through the crowd inside the pub, and several people moved to the door. Someone near the window pointed outside. "Look, a fight."

I scanned the room and didn't see either my mom or dad. Alex was taller than me. "Are they in the back? My parents? Can you see them? Maybe behind the bar?"

"No. I don't see either of them."

I turned and pushed through the crowd to the door with Alex right behind me.

The cool night air washed over me as I threaded my way through the clump of people standing outside the pub's door. I emerged from the crush and saw my dad on his back on the ground, and my mom standing over him with her fists clenched.

CHAPTER 4

The pub didn't have much of an entry area, only a strip of flagstones that formed the sidewalk. I hurried across the area to my dad.

"Mom, how could you?" I squatted down beside my dad. He was already sitting up. Alex went to his other side. I was relieved to see that Mom didn't have the umbrella with her. She must have left it in the pub. I didn't want anyone brandishing umbrellas with lethal points right now.

Mom ignored me and spoke to Dad. "Of all the stupid things to do." Her trembling voice carried through the air, drowning out the sound of a jogger's footfalls as he trotted down the street, his long hair flopping as he ran. "But typical of you. Blundering in where you have no clue and making a mess of things." My words must have finally registered with her because she looked at me suddenly. "How is this my fault?"

"You didn't hit him?" I nodded at the tight ball of her fist as Alex and I reached to help my dad up.

He waved us off. "I'm fine." He got to his feet on his own.

"No, I did not," Mom said. "The very idea. I'm surprised at you, Katherine."

I drew in a deep breath. We were at the full name stage, never a good place to be with a parent.

Dad brushed the tails of his jacket. "No harm done. I just—" He looked at my mom, and some sort of unspoken communication flashed between them. For a second I thought I saw an almost pleading look on Mom's face. Dad adjusted his cuffs. "I tripped. Must be the jet lag. I stepped out for a breath of fresh air, but I'm fine now. Let's all go back inside."

The crowd at the door flowed back inside as Dad moved toward them. Alex and I followed with Mom behind us. Alex and Dad went inside the pub. I stepped back to let my mom go first, but she was looking over her shoulder.

"What's wrong?" I asked.

She whipped her head to me. "Wrong? Not a thing."

"Then what happened? I don't believe for a minute that Dad tripped."

"That's what he said."

"When you trip you fall forward, not backward."

"Did he say tripped? I'm sure he said slipped. Really, you do get worked up over such small things. You always were like that, even as a little girl." She waved for me to go inside first, but I didn't miss the quick glance she gave over her shoulder before she followed me.

~

Ella poked her head in the door of the little room where I was waiting along with my dad, Melissa, and Grace for the musical cue that would signal the beginning of the wedding ceremony. "Tiny little glitch," she said. "The organist is running a few minutes late, but it's okay. We're covered. We have Malcolm."

"I don't understand."

"He plays something like five instruments, including the organ. In an emergency, he can fill in. I'm going to watch for

Sylvia—she's the organist. She swears she'll be here in less than five minutes. I'll hustle her into place the moment she arrives."

Melissa smoothed down a kink in my veil, which I was wearing off my face. It floated in a cloud of tulle behind my head. "Okay," she said, "since we have a few minutes...you have your something old?"

"My gown."

"Something new?"

I lifted the folds of skirt and angled my foot. "Snazzy heels."

"Something borrowed?"

"The veil." It was an antique from Parkview's stash of vintage clothing. Beatrice had stopped by during one of the many planning meetings and mentioned that I was welcome to wear it.

"Something blue?"

"My necklace." I touched the chain and smiled at Grace. She grinned back at me.

"A sixpence in your shoe?"

"What?"

"I thought you might not be prepared for that one. It's part of the rhyme—at least here in England it is. I've got you covered, though." She handed me a silver coin. "It goes in your left shoe for good luck."

I'd never seen a coin like it. "This looks like an antique. Where did you find it?" I balanced on one foot and removed my shoe.

"The Internet, of course."

I tucked the coin into the shoe then worked my foot back into my shoe. The metal felt cold against the sole of my foot. Melissa gave me one last critical survey then nodded. "Perfect."

The notes of the processional floated through the closed door that separated the little room from the Parkview chapel. I looked toward my dad. "Sounds like the organist arrived. It's time."

He straightened his bow tie and came to stand beside me near the door. He may have decided to arrive at the last minute, but he'd had the foresight to bring a tux with him. I had been surprised and touched that he'd thought of that detail. Finding a tux a day before the wedding would have been an almost impossible task.

Grace squeaked and raced into place behind me. Since changing the plans for the seating at the reception had nearly given Malcolm a coronary, we were going mostly with the traditional English way of doing things. Unlike in the States, where the bride entered last, I'd walk up the aisle first with Melissa and Grace behind me.

Dad extended his arm. "Ready?" He peered at my face. "Not having second thoughts?"

I ignored the unsettled feeling in my stomach. Nerves, I told myself. Just the normal jittery feeling you get when you were going to be the center of attention at a once-in-a-lifetime event. "No." In the past I'd been reluctant to analyze my feelings about Alex, but once I'd admitted to myself that I was in love with him I hadn't looked back. Now was not the time to start doubting myself.

"Good. Alex seems like a fine young man. I think you'll do well together."

"Thanks, Dad."

Malcolm swept open the door, nearly snagging my hem. The wiry fringe of his hair shifted around his high forehead in the draft of the door. "We're walking in thirty seconds," he whispered then vanished, leaving the door open. Malcolm had been popping in and out of the room for the last hour. I'd been surprised to find that Ella wasn't kidding about the bow tie. Malcolm had turned up today in a dark tweed jacket, a cream sweater vest, and a black bow tie.

Dad leaned toward me and said in a low voice, "He does realize that those people out there aren't here to see him, right?"

"I think he's using the royal 'we.'"

"As long as he doesn't plan on walking up the aisle then *we're* good." My dad's eyes twinkled with the joke.

I was about to reply, but the music shifted, and Malcolm appeared again with the suddenness of a jack-in-the-box. "Now." He motioned like he was directing traffic and hurried us out the door and into position at the back of the chapel. Once we were in place, he splayed his palms and pressed them to the ground as he whispered, "Slowly. Sedately. Measured."

I wondered distractedly how many more synonyms he could come up with, but then Dad patted my hand on his arm. I took a deep breath. We walked.

CHAPTER 5

I'd been in Parkview's family chapel during tours and admired the wood paneling, the intricate carving of the alabaster altarpiece, and the complex ceiling mural of Christ surrounded with angels in its rich swirl of colors, but I didn't notice any of that now. It was all a blur along with the people in the pews. The queasy feeling intensified, but then my gaze connected with Alex's. It was as if the sea calmed and the horizon leveled. I breathed out and walked on—sedately, of course—but feeling calm and sure. Alex looked more handsome than ever in his tux, but it was the look of love and happiness on his face that I focused on.

Dad patted my hand again when we reached the end of the aisle then went to sit near Mom, who wore the hat we'd found for her a few days ago. With a flat brim broader than the width of her shoulders, the ice blue color matched her dress and sat at an angle on her head. A confection of tulle and feathers on the crown bobbed and shivered with her every movement. Throughout the morning, as she'd zipped back and forth around the tiny anteroom, I felt like we'd been invaded by a tiny blue flying saucer topped with feathers. Tears glistened in her eyes,

44

and I sent her a smile then turned to focus on Alex again so that I didn't get overcome with emotion before the ceremony even began.

Alex and I hadn't wanted a long elaborate service. We had decided we'd have one hymn, *All Things Bright and Beautiful*, and reading from the thirteenth chapter of First Corinthians. The music and words flowed around us and then we said our vows and exchanged rings. It all happened so quickly, it seemed one moment I was reaching for Alex's hand, then a few moments later the final prayer was said, and we kissed—the only amendment we'd made to the traditional service. The wedding ceremony in England doesn't have the "you may kiss the bride" moment, but the vicar had told us it was something that couples often asked to incorporate, so we'd added it. And then we were sweeping down the aisle between the rows of smiling faces as the music swelled.

At the back of the church, we paused, and Malcolm waved us to the door. "To the conservatory. We're running two minutes late."

The conservatory was empty except for a few waiters moving among the linen-covered round tables. Delicate flower arrangements in pink and gold decorated the tables that were laid with shining crystal and silver. I'd kept the decorations simple because no flower arrangement could compete with the elegant room. The ranks of plants that had filled the room during Victorian times had been moved to the greenhouses, and now Parkview used the long room with its soaring ceiling and massive windows as a dining room.

Tall Palladian windows lined one wall and overlooked the gardens. On the other side of the room, a series of niches held Roman statues that various inhabitants of Parkview had brought back from their grand tours of the continent. Several massive stone urns trailing ivy—copies of Greek originals brought back from Rome by the third baronet—filled the spaces between the niches.

Beatrice marched through the tables to us. "Beautiful ceremony. Just beautiful." She was turned out in what she called her "full regalia," a tailored double-breasted dress in royal blue with a matching hat and pumps. Her look today was about as far as you could get from her typical weekday clothes of Wellington boots and a trench coat for trooping through the gardens or plain slacks and a sweater for working in the estate office. Sir Harold, on the other hand, wearing a suit and tie, looked as he always did —formal. He wandered along behind Beatrice, his gaze taking in the place settings and the flowers then drifting to the strings of vintage-style lights that crisscrossed the ceiling. "Nicely done. Just right."

I wasn't sure if he was referring to the ceremony or the decoration of the conservatory, but that was typical for Sir Harold. He always seemed to have his attention focused inward, usually on his projects, which ranged from increasing the estate's honey production to researching the original construction methods used to build Parkview. He'd made sure the restoration project that was underway at the estate would be as authentic as possible.

"So glad you enjoyed it," I said. "Thank you for offering to let us get married here—"

Beatrice waved a hand, cutting me off. "It was our pleasure. Truly, it was. We host so many weddings for strangers. It was a delight to have your ceremony here. Now, we can't stay long. We're off to London for a few days—important meetings with the tourist board—but we wanted to give you our good wishes."

By now, wedding guests were streaming into the room, and Malcolm was hustling back and forth, a worried look on his face as people filtered into seats at the tables. When it was clear that he wouldn't have an angry crowd demanding place cards, he announced, "Family photographs. Can I have Alex's mother, father, and sister? To the terrace, please." Beatrice repeated her good wishes then Malcolm shooed us toward the set of glass doors. Most of the photos from the wedding day would be informal ones, capturing candid moments, but we also wanted a handful of group photos of our families.

Our photographer was set up outside so that the lush gardens would be the background of the photo. Alex's dad and Grace arrived first, then a slender woman with an emerald green fascinator hat positioned so that it dipped over one eye approached.

"Alex, darling," she called, "you must introduce me to your little bride." From a distance, I could tell she was a beautiful woman with platinum blond hair and a curvy figure. As she got closer, I noticed the tightness of the dress, the artificial smoothness of the skin around her eyes and forehead, and the odd protrusion of her lips that made me think of a cartoon duck. She leaned in so Alex could kiss her cheek, but she didn't have to pinch her lips—they seemed to be permanently stuck in a puckering position. She playfully tapped him on the shoulder. "So naughty of you not to have introduced us earlier."

"I would have loved to, but you showed up a few minutes before the ceremony started." Alex's voice held a note of disapproval.

"Oh, don't pout. I made it with two minutes to spare. You know I never spend a moment longer in a church than I absolutely have to."

A muscle worked in Alex's jaw. "It's so nice to meet you, Mrs. Norcutt," I said quickly.

"Call me Lexi, darling. Oh, hello, Grace. Don't you look like a sweet little princess," she added. Grace flushed.

Didn't Lexi realize that calling a thirteen-year-old a little princess was not a good move? At thirteen, you wanted to be thought of as mature and grown-up. Fortunately, the photographer called for us to move to the stone balustrade. The next quarter hour was spent posing and smiling, first with Alex's family, then with mine. When my parents came out for their photos, my dad pumped Alex's hand then gave him a cigar while my mom fluttered around me. "Such a gorgeous ceremony. I knew it would be unique and charming. Just unforgettable."

"I'm glad you enjoyed it, Mom." I really meant it. My mom had been looking forward to my wedding day for years—more often than I had looked forward to it—and I'd been worried that no matter how nice the ceremony was it wouldn't live up to her expectations.

"Oh, I did. It was amazing. Yes, I'll shush," she said to the photographer. "I know we have to take the photos."

After the photos, we sat down to the wedding breakfast, which wasn't breakfast at all. It was called that because it was the first meal that we ate as husband and wife. I'd called it the wedding reception because that's how I thought of it, and since I continually spoke of it that way, Malcolm had begun to use the same term. I think it was to humor me—one of those keep-the-bride-happy-at-all-costs kind of things—but I'd noticed that it had rubbed off on my other friends, and now it was the "reception," not the "breakfast."

Between the toasts and talking with the guests seated on each side of us, Alex and I didn't eat much. He leaned toward me as the plates for the last course were whisked away. "I think we may need to pick up some Chinese food on the way to the cottage, Mrs. Norcutt."

"That sounds odd."

"Chinese?"

"No. The fact that I'm Mrs. Norcutt. It's just—weird. Good, but strange."

A sudden squawking sound cut through the air, and everyone looked to the back of the room where Ella was walking rapidly toward a young woman with straight dark hair that fell below her shoulders. Dark brows slashed across her forehead. She wore a denim jacket and jeans and was pointing at someone at a back table as she shrieked.

"What's she saying?" I asked Alex. "Can you make it out?"

"No idea."

Ella reached her, wrapped an arm around the woman's shoulders, and propelled her out the door.

A moment of silence stretched for a second then a wave of conversation rolled across the room, again filling the air along with the clink of silverware on china.

"I wonder who that was?" I mentally scrolled through the invitation list. We'd opted out of a receiving line, but had circulated through the room before taking our seat at the head table. I didn't remember seeing the woman with the documentary crew or either one of our families.

"She didn't look familiar to me either," Alex said.

"And she didn't look like she was dressed for the wedding." My mother had been right. Most of the women had worn hats along with their best "frocks," as Melissa called them.

Alex said, "Malcolm's signaling. Must be time for the cake."

We cut the cake, smiled for more pictures, and even had time to eat a few bites. I put down my fork. "I'm going to talk to Grace. I want to return the necklace before she has to leave. Malcolm's keeping us on a pretty tight schedule, and I don't want to forget."

Alex said, "Good idea. Dad is good at staying on time so they'll be out of here soon."

Randall had several days off before he had to return to Chile. He was taking Grace on a trip to Disneyland Paris, and they were leaving tonight after the reception.

I unhooked the opal necklace then crouched down beside Grace, who was seated at the end of the head table because she was part of the wedding party. "Thank you for letting me borrow the necklace." I dropped it into her palm. "I wanted to make sure you got it back before you left. Are you excited about the trip?"

"Yeah, it'll be fun. We're going to ride the biggest roller coasters first. We've already decided."

"Good plan." I couldn't help smiling at the thought of distinguished Randall with his hands in the air in a roller-coaster car.

"Dad loves coasters."

"Does he?"

She nodded. "My mom, not so much."

I didn't find that hard to believe at all, but I kept the thought to myself.

"Oh, I found a new mystery author," Grace said. "I mean, she's not new-new. She's new to me."

One of the things that Grace and I had bonded over was our shared love of mysteries, in particular, Miss Marple.

"Her name is Dorothy L. Sayers," Grace said.

"Really?" I asked, surprised. "I've read some of her novels. I would have thought they'd be kind of...hard going." I didn't add for a thirteen-year-old.

She wrinkled her nose. "Some parts are, but I just skip those. Lord Peter and Bunter are so funny. One of the books is about a honeymoon. Have you read it?"

"No, I don't think so."

"*Busman's Honeymoon.* Maybe you should get it before you leave."

"Good idea. I'll make sure I download a copy. We're flying, so I'm packing light. I better get back. I think it's almost time for dancing."

As I walked to my seat, I glanced at the end of the room where the band was arranging music on stands. I slipped back into my seat beside Alex. "The band is setting up."

"That's a pity," Alex whispered. His breath feathered over my bare shoulder, sending interesting little ripples through me. "I hoped they wouldn't show up. I was all for making our escape early."

"We can't do that—yet," I said, and Alex sent me a look that made me wish we were completely alone. "But I think a few dances are all that's required."

"Excellent." Alex stood and held out his hand. "It looks like Malcolm is motioning for us. Shall we dance and then depart?"

"Definitely."

Of course it wasn't quite that simple. We actually danced to quite a few songs. Alex and I had our dance, then I danced with my dad, and Alex danced with his mom. Later, I saw Alex's mom, Lexi, swaying with my dad, who had a bemused expression on his face. Louise, in Carl's arms, looked happier than I'd ever seen her. She caught my eye over Carl's shoulder and gave me an exaggerated wink. My mom's flying saucer hat rotated around the dance floor. I even saw her dancing with Malcolm and decided I should overlook his fussiness from now on.

The music shifted from romantic to upbeat pop rock. Across the dance floor, Alex's gaze connected with mine. He raised an eyebrow. I nodded. I was dancing with Brent who was saying, "... and then Alex decided it wouldn't be that hard to jump from one balcony to the other at the ski lodge. If he was going to do it, I was too. Alex, being Alex, did flawlessly."

"I bet you did, too."

Brent shook his head. "Nope. Broke my leg."

I winced. Alex heard the last part of the conversation as he approached. "I knew it would be the balcony story," Alex said. "Did he tell you that I was grounded from the slopes for the rest of the winter?"

"I'm sure he was getting to it." I glanced between the two of them. Clearly, it was a story that had been told and retold and there were no hard feelings about the incident now.

"And we were in Austria at the time," Alex added.

"A punishment worse than death for Alex," Brent said.

"I can imagine," I said. Alex had put winter sports on the back burner for now, but I knew he'd been quite good at snow-boarding.

"Okay enough stories." Alex tapped Brent on the shoulder. "Cutting in on you. Husband's prerogative."

Brent stepped back with a flourish, and Alex and I danced off the floor. Ella broke off her conversation with a young woman to introduce us. "This is Sylvia McNamee, our organist."

Sylvia turned to us. "I was apologizing to Ella, but I should be saying it to you. I'm sorry that I cut it so close today. I had a flat tire and had to get a ride." She wore a plainly cut navy dress and a tiny fascinator with only one small flower accent. The nondescript nature of her clothes didn't make her look dowdy. Instead, they highlighted her beauty. Her rich honey-colored hair was swept back in a simple knot, which accented her high cheekbones, creamy skin, and large brown eyes.

"No worries. It all worked out," Alex said, and I nodded my agreement.

"I'll get out of your way," Sylvia said to us. "Nice to meet you both," she added before merging back into the crowd.

Ella turned to us. "You're leaving?"

Alex nodded, and I said, "That won't throw things off, will it?"

"Nope, I knew you'd be ready to go early. Your car awaits." She gestured out the window where Alex's MG sat on one of the wide gravel paths with a "Just Married" sign hanging off the back along with ribbons and tin cans attached to the back bumper. "Your bags are packed and in the car. You can change into your going-away clothes. We have everything waiting for you. You're in the little salon, Kate. Alex, I'm sorry, but the grooms get what is basically a converted storage room." Ella pointed to the opposite side of the conservatory. "Leave your wedding clothes in the rooms. We'll make sure everything is cleaned and returned."

I changed into a smart little suit that Melissa had helped me find then hung up the wedding dress and carefully smoothed down the folds. I'd loved wearing it. I'd actually felt rather princess-like in it. I'd enjoyed the ceremony and the celebration with family and friends, but I was ready to be alone with Alex.

I returned to the conservatory where Alex was waiting for me dressed in a plain white button down shirt, dress pants, and a jacket—still dressed up for him, but not nearly as fancy as his tux. Malcolm was lining up the guests, creating a corridor for us. "Ready to go?" he asked.

"Yes."

Alex squeezed my hand, and we jogged to the car with rose petals and confetti raining on us.

~

"I'm all for going back to bed," Alex said, sending me a look that made my insides go as fluttery as they had before the wedding ceremony yesterday, but this time the feeling had nothing to do with nerves. The tiny round table in the kitchen of Cart Cottage was crowded with a vase of white and pink mums—a present from Parkview's staff—and the remains of our late breakfast. We'd decided to skip the Chinese food last night after all, and had driven straight to Cart Cottage after we left Parkview. We'd hardly stirred from the little bedroom upstairs until late this morning.

"We've only just gotten *out* of bed. We've been terrible sluggish. It's nearly noon." I slathered some clotted cream onto my last bite of scone and popped it in my mouth.

"We're on our honeymoon. We're supposed to be sluggards."

"Good point. I could probably be persuaded..."

"I hope I win all our arguments that easily—"

A knock sounded on the door of the little cottage. I frowned. Alex looked at me, his eyebrows raised.

"I didn't tell anyone we'd be here." I'd made sure that I didn't mention our stay in Cart Cottage to anyone, and I thought Alex had probably kept our itinerary quiet, too. "It can't be my mom," I said. "She was leaving for Manchester early this morning for a tour." Even before the wedding, she had been busily planning her schedule for the rest of her time in England, packing in as many tours and sightseeing trips as she could during the week after the wedding before her return flight to California.

Alex stood. "I had a text from my dad. He and Grace are already in France. They landed last night." Alex walked to the door. "And I know my mom planned to leave after the reception last night, too. She wouldn't stick around. I'm sure she was in London before midnight."

I followed him, wiping my fingers on a napkin.

Constable Albertson stood outside, the lines on his craggy face looking more deeply etched in the bright sunlight. "Sorry to disturb, but we have a...situation at Parkview."

"What sort of situation?" I asked, my stomach suddenly churning. All of our close friends and relatives had been at Parkview.

"A murder."

The napkin fluttered to the ground.

"Who?" asked Alex as he put his arm around my shoulders.

Constable Albertson scratched his hairline, pushing his hat back an inch. "That's the problem. We don't know who it is."

CHAPTER 6

*C*onstable Albertson repositioned his hat. "Hate to intrude on you at this time, but the DCI thinks you're the best option for identification. No wallet or phone was found, and the DCI wants to nail down ID as soon as possible."

"They're sure it isn't someone from Parkview? An employee possibly?" Alex asked.

"No, he isn't one of the staff. But he did have a menu card from the breakfast—I mean the reception, as you call it, so probably a guest. We need one of you to take a look, so you can tell us who he is."

My stomach lurched as I thought of our families and most of our friends who had come to the wedding.

"I'll go," Alex said.

"I'm coming too."

Alex opened his mouth and I could tell he was going to argue, but he took one look at my face, and said, "You don't have to."

"Yes, I do. I can't sit around here and wait."

Alex reached for my hand. "No, that wouldn't be like you at all."

~

From the moment we passed through Parkview's gates, the stately home had a completely different atmosphere than it had the day before. Yesterday white ribbons and tiny pink flowers had adorned the stone pillars on each side of the wrought-iron gates. Today the decorations were gone, and a police car blocked the drive.

Several police vehicles were parked on the gravel sweep in front of the house, one of them with the words "Crime Scene Investigation" printed on the side. A group of people near it were taking off their white jumpsuits, which had covered every inch of their bodies, except their faces. A few had already stripped off gloves and face masks while others balanced on one foot as they removed booties. The protective gear looked especially odd against the background of the classical lines of the building and the spreading grounds of Parkview.

Constable Albertson motioned for us to follow him around the side of the house. Instead of wedding guests in pretty dresses and hats, police moved back and forth through the banks of flowers in the gardens.

"It's a bit of a hike," Albertson said as we climbed the path that left the formal gardens and crested the low rise of hill behind the house. Once we reached the top, the extent of Parkview's grounds was visible, stretching into the distance, still green, but with flashes of fall colors touching the trees.

A man-made lake reflected the clear sky. Beyond it stood the folly, a round open-air building with six columns and a domed ceiling. Crime scene tape ringed the empty benches spaced around the folly. Another section of tape cordoned off the area to the right of the folly, the shrubbery maze. A uniformed officer stood at the entrance to the maze. The hedge towered over him, making him look like a miniature figure against the wall of greenery. If you were on ground level at the maze you couldn't see anyone once they went inside. It was only here on the elevated ground that I could see a few tiny figures as they moved through the turns of the maze.

We fell into single file to let a police officer pass us as we made our way around the lake. As we neared the maze, my heart beat faster, and my stomach felt worse. When Albertson said a man had been killed, my thoughts had immediately gone to the worst possible outcome—a family member or close friend—but Alex's quiet presence had steadied me. I'd forced myself not to run through the possibilities of who the dead man could be, but now with the crime scene tape and the somber quiet, my anxiety was rising.

I felt Alex's gaze on me as he came alongside me again. I reached for his hand, which felt like an anchor in a world that was suddenly tilting crazily. "Bit of an unusual situation, bringing us out here, isn't it?" Alex asked Albertson as we followed him along the descending path. I threw Alex a small smile. He was trying to distract me, and I appreciated the effort, but nothing was going to take away the uneasiness I felt.

"It is," Albertson said, "but the medical examiner is tied up with a bad crash near Ashfield. Coach overturned. He wants this body left as it is until he can get here and see it, but the DCI wants to get moving with the investigation. Guests are scheduled to checkout today. He's holding everyone now until we know more about the victim, but some people are already gone."

We reached a section of tape that enclosed both the folly and the maze, and paused while Constable Albertson let someone know he was bringing Alex and me into the crime scene. "A gardener found him this morning." Albertson lifted the tape, and we ducked under it.

"Do they think he's been there all night?" I asked, trying to work out if anyone had left the reception before we did.

"I don't know. I was tasked with getting you."

"I suppose one of the wedding guests could have come out

here yesterday," I said. "All the activities were in the house, but there was nothing preventing anyone from leaving the reception and strolling through the gardens and grounds."

Albertson said, "You should mention that to DCI Quimby."

I absorbed the fact that it was Detective Chief Inspector Quimby in charge of the investigation. I'd met him before, and I knew he was thorough. We walked on in silence, the only sound the muted voice of someone in the maze. When we reached the entrance to the maze, Albertson nodded at the officer stationed there, then escorted us inside. I'd been in the maze before, but had never moved through it so quickly. Then I noticed that as we made our way through the twists and turns, a piece of crime scene tape had been tied off in the hedges at each intersection, indicating the correct direction to turn. We reached the center of the maze, a circular area with a fountain in the middle, which was now dry. Even without water spraying, the fountain was beautiful and would usually have been the focus of the little area, but I barely glanced at it. My attention went immediately to the area on the side of the fountain where a canopy had been put up. I could see a figure on the ground, but the shade made it hard to distinguish any details, and an officer blocked my view of the man's face.

Quimby, who was dressed in his typical shade of nondescript brown, was under the canopy but came across to meet Alex and me as soon as he saw us.

"I understand congratulations are in order." He shook first Alex's hand then mine.

"Yes," Alex said. "It's official. We're an old married couple now."

"Best wishes to you. I apologize for asking you to come out here, on today of all days, but—well—you're the best choice to give us the information we need."

I forced myself to look away from the body under the canopy to Quimby. "We'll help in any way we can."

Quimby said, "Thank you. If you'll come with me."

We crossed the grassy area and stopped at the edge of the canopy. It took a minute for my eyes to adjust to the dimness after the bright sunlight.

A young man, probably in his mid-twenties, lay on his back, one arm flung out from his side. The metal hilt of a knife protruded from his chest. Hardly any blood had seeped into his white dress shirt. His dark suit jacket was completely free of blood. I managed to draw my gaze away from the knife and studied the man's pale face.

Beside me, Alex said, "No, I'm sorry. I have no idea who he is. Never seen him before. Are you sure he was at the wedding?"

I felt a rush of relief that it wasn't my dad or a close friend from the documentary crew, then immediately felt guilty—someone else wouldn't be so lucky and would get terrible news soon. Then I blinked and looked closer. Suddenly, I wished I hadn't been so accommodating earlier. If only I'd stayed back at the cottage...

"Ms. Sharp—er, I, pardon me. "Mrs. Norcutt?" Quimby asked.

"What?"

"Do you know him?"

"No, I don't." I debated leaving it at that. Quimby let out a barely audible sigh.

The man's face was slack. Maybe I was wrong...? But the hair. Long on top, short on the side...and the beard. Death had changed his appearance, but not so much that I didn't recognize him.

I took a deep breath and, after a quick glance at Alex, I said to Quimby, "I don't know him, but I think I've seen him before, in the airport when I picked up my mom last week."

CHAPTER 7

*Q*uimby's eyebrows flared up. "So, you agree, not a wedding guest?"

"No, definitely not," I said. Our wedding guests had been our family and close friends. I knew every name on the list. Everyone I hadn't known personally before the wedding, like Brent, I'd met and spoken with sometime during the last few days.

Quimby removed his phone from his pocket and poised his fingers to make a note. "Which airport did your mother arrive at?"

Before I could answer, his phone rang. He read the caller ID. "I have to take this," he said and stepped back from us. After a few moments, he pulled the phone away from his ear and motioned Albertson over. "Take them back to Parkview," he said with a nod in our direction. "I have a few more questions for them, but I have to handle this call. Coordinate a place in the house where we can do interviews. And find Mrs. Sharp—the mother. I want to talk to her next."

As Alex and I followed Albertson through the break in the tall hedge, I said, "My mother is in Manchester today. At least, that was her plan yesterday."

"Where exactly?"

"Um...all over the city, I think. She's on a tour."

Albertson said, "Okay, we'll have to wait until she gets back, I suppose. How did she get to Manchester? Does she have a car?"

"No—that could be disastrous."

Albertson smiled briefly at my reaction to his question. "Not comfortable with driving on the left?"

"Definitely not. Parkview arranged transportation for her, a private car, I think. Malcolm or Ella will know. I can text Mom, but I don't know if she'll reply. She usually doesn't keep her phone on."

"No need. I'll track down the car service."

We emerged from the walls of the maze and moved back through the taped off areas. As we hiked around the lake, up the hill, and through the gardens I could feel Alex's gaze on me. I looked at Albertson's back and mouthed the words, *"Tell you later."* Alex nodded, but he looked worried.

Once back in the house, Albertson consulted with Malcolm, who met us in the entry hall, his face somber as he smoothed down his fringe hair. "It's ghastly. Just ghastly," Malcolm muttered as he crossed the black-and-white tiled floor. "So upsetting for Lady Stone. I spoke with her on the phone. She's extremely shocked and sends her deepest condolences to...the family of the...er, person."

Malcolm sounded like a press release and, while I knew Beatrice would be concerned about the incident, I thought Malcolm was probably exaggerating her emotional reaction.

We followed him into the library as he said, "She's quite distraught. She's so protective of the estate. To have—er, violence —intrude here..."

Albertson said, "Quite." He looked around the spacious book-lined room. "This will be fine."

Malcolm tugged at the hem of his vest. "Lady Stone instructed me to tell you to take as much time as you need. Please let us know if there is anything we can do."

"Thank you." Albertson's tone indicated dismissal, but Malcolm lingered. "Is there any word...on the identity of the... um...unfortunate person?"

"Not at this time," Albertson said. He didn't glance at me.

"I see." Malcolm went to the door. "Please ring the bell if you need anything." He pointed to the bell pull, then closed the door.

Albertson followed Malcolm to the door as he said, "I'll go find out about your mum."

"Do you think it was a robbery?" I asked Albertson.

The constable paused. "It's possible, but it's too early to tell," he said and went out.

I dropped down onto the couch facing the floor-to-ceiling windows that looked out on the drive. Alex sat down beside me, eyebrows raised. I sagged back against the soft cushions with a shrug.

It was true, what everyone said about married couples, that they could communicate without words. Alex had always been able to read me pretty well—he was much more intuitive than I was—but we both seemed to have stepped up a level in the nonverbal-communications arena.

"You're worried," Alex said.

"Yes. There's no reason to be. That man is probably some stranger Mom chatted with at the airport while she waited for me to get back, but..." I tucked my hair behind my ears and sat up straighter. "She acted strange at the airport and in the car. She didn't want to talk about it. She was secretive, and that's never good."

"Are you going to tell Quimby?"

"About my mom acting odd? No. My mom can tell him herself what happened. I only have my feelings, my observation, of what happened. Quimby will want facts."

"Did you see the man's watch?" Alex asked.

"I didn't notice it. At first I couldn't look away from the knife —I've never seen anything like that—and, then when I managed to look at his face…I was so surprised that he looked familiar that I didn't notice anything else."

"It looked like a Skagen."

"What's that?"

"A watch brand."

"I've never heard of it."

"It's not incredibly expensive, but still a nice watch. It probably cost over a hundred dollars."

"Oh. So maybe it wasn't a robbery." I realized I was twisting my wedding ring around my finger and dropped my hands to my lap. "Maybe this death is one of those extraordinary coincidences that happen sometimes."

"A person your mother met randomly at the airport shows up dead after our wedding—and neither one of us knew him?"

"No, you're right." I closed my eyes for a second. Goodbye, uninterrupted days holed up in the cottage with Alex. Goodbye, honeymoon. "It's *too* extraordinary. It can't be a coincidence."

～

We had a long wait in the library. Mostly, Alex and I sat in silence, holding hands, my gaze roving over the gold-lettered titles. I jumped at every noise from the front of the house, but none of them were Mom arriving back. Eventually, the caravan of official vehicles left Parkview, including a medical examiner's van.

When Quimby finally came in the library, he apologized for the long wait, and said he had a few more questions about my identification of the man.

I wasn't sure "man at the airport" constituted an identification, but apparently it was all the investigators had to work with at this point.

Quimby settled at a large desk with leather inlays. He waved Alex and me into the chairs on the other side of the desk as he asked, "You picked up your mother Wednesday?"

"Yes, that's right," I said. "I don't have her flight number, but I'm sure she can get it for you when she gets back." I glanced out the windows, but the sweep in front of the house and the drive that curved into the woods remained empty except for one car, which I assumed was the one Quimby had arrived in.

"There's no need for that. We can track it down." He dialed a number, repeated the information, and added, "And have someone check the inn, see if anyone matching the description was staying there. If he wasn't, branch out from there and cover the surrounding hotels and bed and breakfasts...right. Keep me updated."

Quimby checked his watch. "Your mother should be here soon. Constable Albertson was able to track her driver. He had his mobile on and said he should be back within the hour. Now, about the man in the maze," he said, and I couldn't help but think that it sounded like a mystery novel title. Quimby must have had the same thought because he paused and gave a small shake of his head, then said in a low voice, "I hope the papers don't get ahold of this. They won't be able to resist a phrase like that." His voice returned to normal as he asked, "I realize you said the man wasn't a wedding guest, but did either of you see our John Doe at the wedding or the breakfast—er, the reception, I believe you're calling it?"

"No, I didn't," I said.

Alex echoed my words, then asked, "Are you sure he was there?"

"Because he had the menu card in his pocket, at this point, we have to assume he was there, even if no one recognizes him. Did you have any extra seats? Could he have slipped into a seat without a place card?"

"We did have extra open seats. I made sure we had about six extra places, just in case. And a few people weren't able to come at the last minute, so I'd say we probably had ten empty seats. But we didn't have place cards. It was open seating. If he did slip in somehow, then he could have picked any chair without drawing attention to himself."

"Maybe someone gave him the menu card after the wedding," Alex said.

It was a good point, and I liked it because it removed the wedding in general—and my mom in particular—from the equation.

"That is possible, of course," Quimby said. "But looking at the initial time of death estimate, it doesn't seem likely."

"You think he died sometime during the night?" I asked.

"Yes. As a matter of form, where were both of you last night between midnight and two in the morning?"

"Cart Cottage," I said.

Alex added, "Together, the whole time," and I felt a blush creep into my face.

Quimby made a note in his phone and murmured, "I should hope so." Then he said, "And then we have his clothes to consider. A suit and tie, which may indicate he was at a formal event."

He had been wearing a dark suit and tie along with a white shirt. Perfect attire for a wedding.

"Except for his shoes," Alex said.

Quimby nodded. "Yes, trainers are rather informal for a suit."

"He had on tennis shoes?" I asked Alex.

"Neon green and blue," Alex said. "They didn't go with the rest of his clothes."

"I completely missed that." I had been so focused on the knife that I hadn't even looked at the man's feet.

The door flew open, and Mom burst into the room. "A murder? Can it be true?" She wore a sun visor, a windbreaker, jeans, and tennis shoes. She swung her umbrella, jabbing it into the Axminster rug with each step. She now wore her money belt on the outside of her clothes like a fanny pack, but it was positioned over her hip. A thick guidebook stuck out of it, and the whole thing thumped against her hip as she strode across the room to us.

"I'm afraid it is, Mom. But we're all okay."

"Here, have my seat, Mrs. Sharp," Alex said.

She transferred all her attention to him. "Gallant boy. So glad you're here to take care of Kate at a time like this." She patted his shoulder before taking his chair.

"Mom, this is Detective Chief Inspector Quimby." I wished I could somehow warn her about the questions he'd surely ask her. I had a bad feeling about the whole situation.

"Oh, I didn't even see you there." She shifted away from Alex and me toward the desk. "It's so dim in that corner. You practically blend in with the books. Inspector? A real-life inspector like the one in Sherlock Holmes, Inspector Lestrade?"

"Not quite," Quimby said, and I could tell he wasn't flattered by the comparison. I couldn't say that I blamed him. Lestrade wasn't exactly known for his brilliant crime-solving skills. "I'm not fictional," Quimby said. "I have a few questions for you."

Mom blinked. "For me? Why me?"

Quimby held out his phone to Mom. "Do you recognize this man?"

I caught a glimpse of the image as he passed it over. It was a photo of the dead man's face, probably taken while he was still on the ground in the maze because I could see the background of green, the grass behind his head.

Mom took the phone. After a tiny pause, she said, "No, no idea," in her falsely bright voice that brought back memories of the aftermath of fights between her and dad. *No, dear, everything is fine.* And I didn't miss the slight narrowing of her eyes before she opened them wide and went into her clueless act.

Quimby didn't miss the hesitation. "You're sure?"

"Yes, of course." She held out the phone, but Quimby didn't take it.

"Look closely. It's an official inquiry in a homicide investigation. Your daughter recognized him, and says you talked with the man."

Mom shot me a look. I could tell she was longing to break into full-name territory and call me "Katherine." But her gaze flicked to Quimby then back to the phone. She frowned at the image for a moment then cleared her throat. "Perhaps. He's dead? He's the murdered one?"

"Yes," Quimby said.

I could have sworn that a look of relief chased across mom's face for a split second before she shrugged. "I don't know. I mean, I've met so many people here in the last few days—all of them new to me..." She placed the phone on the desk since Quimby still hadn't reached for it. He didn't say anything else, just kept staring at her.

She gripped the arms of the chair and prepared to stand. "Is that all? It's been an exhausting day. So interesting, though. I saw the cathedral, a canal, and a rebuilt Roman fort. Then it was on to a museum with a display of the actual sheet music from one of the The Edge of Zero's original songs. Remember, Kate, I told you we might be related to Tom Davis through your father's side—"

"Mom." My tone startled her. I pushed the phone back toward her. The image had gone dark, so I touched the screen. "At the airport? Don't you remember? He was at the airport."

She studied my face for a second then removed her hands from the chair arms. She transferred her gaze to the phone and studied it for a long moment. "The young man at the coffee shop, you mean? I *suppose* that could be him."

"Now that your daughter has jogged your memory," Quimby said with a look at me that signaled I should stop interfering, "what can you tell me about him?"

"Tell you? Nothing. We only chatted about—flying...you know how it is. How you never know if your checked bags will actually show up, that sort of thing."

"Did he introduce himself?"

"No."

"Did he mention where he'd traveled from?"

Mom shook her head.

Quimby persisted. "Or where he was going?"

"No, I told you. It was vague small talk. Nothing specific or detailed. I'm sorry I can't help you, but there it is." She stood. "The tour was quite long. I never realized Manchester was so large. So nice to meet you. Now, I must change for dinner."

Quimby opened his mouth, and I was sure he was about to order my mother back to the chair, but then he saw the name of the incoming call on his phone. "Let me know if you remember anything else. Your daughter knows how to get in touch with me."

~

"Whatever did he mean by that?" Mom asked as soon as we were out of the library.

"I couldn't say." I shot a look at Alex to make sure he wasn't about to clue my mom in on my past involvement in a few police investigations. I'd intentionally avoided telling her the details of some of them and had even glossed over a few completely. I certainly didn't want to get into that now.

As we climbed the steps to the next floor where the guest bedrooms were located, Alex whispered, "*I'm* not going there."

I slowed, letting my mom trot a few steps ahead so she wouldn't overhear as I spoke to Alex. "Turnabout is fair play. I can keep a secret as well as she can—and that's what she's doing. She knows something about that man, but she's trying to pretend that she doesn't. If I can get her alone, I might be able to find out what it is."

Alex paused as we came to the landing at the top of the stairs. "Okay, I'll disappear for a while—" A door down the hall opened, and my dad stepped out of his room. He'd moved to Parkview two nights ago, and I was pleased to see he hadn't moved back to the inn immediately after the wedding. He was also staying another week in England. He said it was so he could do some sightseeing and visit bookshops, but I thought it might have more to do with putting off the return flight to the States. He'd talked about switching to a cruise ship, but hadn't changed his travel plans yet.

He nodded to my mom as she passed him. She inclined her head in a way that would have looked regal if she hadn't been wearing a sun visor with the words "Manchester United" on it.

He didn't look surprised to see us as he joined us on the landing. "Bad business, this murder."

"You know about that?" I asked. "I thought you were going to visit all the bookshops today."

"I did. Went out this morning and got a nice haul. Nothing spectacular, but several interesting things. I found a book of antique maps. Excellent condition. The trouble is the time change. I can't seem to adjust. I was up half the night, then I finally got to sleep, but in a few hours, it was light, and I can't sleep once the sun is up. I went out early, but after a few hours, I nearly fell asleep, waiting to pay for my books in a little shop in Upper Benning. That's when I decided to call it a day and came back in a taxi. Slept like a baby on the way back, only to find the police blocking the gates. Had to prove I was a guest here before they'd let me in."

SARA ROSETT

He tilted his head toward his room. "I spent the afternoon watching the comings and goings from my window." His room was situated on the east side of the house. From his windows, he'd have an uninterrupted view of the gardens to the lake beyond the little hill. You could even see the folly from those rooms. "Bad business," he repeated as he rubbed his eyes. "Listen to me, going on. Why are you here? I thought you two were staying in some undisclosed location, a little cottage I heard, until it's time for your flight to Italy."

"We would be, except the police asked us to identify the man they found because they thought he was a wedding guest," I said.

My dad fell back a step. "That's terrible. Was it someone...?"

"No one we knew," I said quickly. "At least, no one Alex and I knew, but I think Mom talked to him at the airport. I'm on my way to get the real story out of her."

Alex said, "I'll wait for you here."

"Good choice." Dad nodded to the billiard table visible through an open door. "I want to try that out. No idea how to play the game, but it seems to me that if you're staying in an English country house, you should at least give billiards a try." He asked Alex, "Care to join me?"

"No idea how to play either, but I'll give it a go."

I left them discussing whether they should look up the official rules on Alex's phone or just play a modified version of pool.

I knocked on the door of Mom's room. "It's me, Mom."

Her muted voice sounded through the door. "It's unlocked."

I stepped inside. She'd removed the visor, changed into a robe, and was sitting at a little dressing table touching up her makeup. "Hello, dear." Her words were distorted as she flexed her lips to apply a fresh coat of lipstick.

I dragged a chair covered in green-and-white striped silk over to the dressing table and positioned it so that I could see her face. "Mom, you need to tell me what you know about the guy at the airport."

She kept her gaze on the mirror as she put the lipstick away then removed a fleck of mascara from under an eye. "I don't know anything about him."

"I don't believe you."

"Kate, you're doing it again—getting worked up over nothing. You should be with Alex. It's the first day of your honeymoon." She picked up a makeup brush and swept it over her cheeks.

It took some effort, but I ignored her and stayed focused. "You know why I don't believe you? I know when you're lying. I can tell. You get this squinty look for a second, then you delve into your what-are-you-talking-about act. But that's what it is, an act."

She threw down the brush and shifted so that she faced me. "It's not important."

"It's a *murder* investigation. Do you know what Quimby is going to do? He's going to take what you told him and check it. He'll try and pick it apart."

She shoved the chair back and went across to the large wardrobe where she jerked the doors open. "So I talked to Nick at the airport. So what?"

"Nick?"

She sighed and pulled out a dress in a leopard print material. "Yes, his name was Nick."

"Nick. Okay, good. Did he tell you his last name?"

"Davis." She selected a pair of black pumps with leopard print bows as well as a pair of black flats. Looking between the two pairs of shoes, she said, "So the most they'll find out is that I talked to him a few times." She held up the shoes with the bows against the dress. "What do you think? Too much?"

"You talked to him more than once?"

She waved both the shoes and the dress in a no-big-deal motion. "We met a couple of times for coffee. It was nothing more than that."

I swallowed the sudden lump in my throat. "You mean...you knew him in California?"

"Yes, that's what I said. Weren't you listening? You really should pay closer attention, especially since *you're* the one going on and on with the questions."

I rubbed my forehead. "This is so much worse than I thought."

CHAPTER 8

"How can a few innocent meetings—it was only a cup of coffee occasionally—be bad?" Mom asked as she set the shoes with the bows down and returned the other pair to the wardrobe.

"Mom." I rubbed my forehead. I had that pulsing feeling in my temples that meant a headache might be coming on. "It's bad. Trust me." I hopped up, caught her shoulders, and then drew her down to sit on the bed beside me. "You lied to the police. Once they figure that out, they'll doubt everything you tell them. You'll no longer be an innocent person on the edge of an investigation. You'll be someone they can't trust, and they'll look at you more closely."

"Surely not," she said, but some of the confidence had drained from her tone. She adjusted the folds of her robe. "It will be fine. They'll find out I sent him a letter, and we had a few meetings. That was it, until I happened to run into him at the airport."

"You sent him a letter?" I latched on to the strangest thing in her narrative. Who sends letters these days?

"Yes. For my family tree. I was looking for Nick Davis, a descendant of Tom Davis, the singer I told you about? With such a common name, it's not easy. You have to kiss a lot of frogs before you find a prince in genealogical research, let me tell you."

I blinked, working out the metaphor. "You mean, you contacted several people named Nick Davis?"

"Exactly!" She shifted into a more comfortable position on the bed. "What you do, you see, is there are all these marvelous databases—"

"Mom, please, let's just focus on this Nick Davis. Why did you send him the letter?"

"Because he was one of the names that came up. I'd had no luck tracing Rebecca Westings—she married Tom and took his name—but then Nick's name came up. Sometimes you can reach people through the Internet, but sometimes I've had better luck with actual letters. So unusual now to get a real letter—that's why I think it works so well. I couldn't find an email for this Nick Davis, but I had an address in San Bernardino, which isn't that far from me. On the off chance that he might be *the* Nick Davis whose mother was Rebecca Westings, who was married to Tom Davis, I sent him a letter and gave him my phone number."

My head was spinning with all the names, but I focused on the one important fact. "And he called you?" I asked, my thoughts skipping ahead. When the police found Nick's phone or got his phone records, my mother's number would be in his call log.

"Yes, right away. I was delighted," she said, then her bright face saddened. "But he was the *wrong* Nick Davis. With two names that are so common, I shouldn't have been disappointed, but he could tell I was disheartened. Common names make it so difficult. Anyway, he offered to buy me a coffee to cheer me up."

"And you met him? A stranger that you knew nothing about?" I realized I sounded more like a mom than a daughter, but I couldn't help it.

"In broad daylight in a busy coffee shop. What could happen there?"

"That's not the attitude you'd have if our situations were

reversed." I thought of all the lectures and warnings she gave me as a teen.

"Well, nothing happened. He was charming and *so* interested in genealogy."

"That doesn't seem like something a guy in his twenties would be into."

"Just because you're not interested in it doesn't mean no one else is. It's fascinating. Anyway, he was thinking of tracing his own family tree and wanted to know how to go about it."

"So you talked to him about genealogy. What else?"

"You'd sent me a picture of your wedding dress, and I couldn't resist showing it to him. He wanted to hear all the details about the wedding."

"That seems odd." I tried to picture Alex buying coffee for a middle-aged woman and being interested in the details of her daughter's destination wedding...nope. I didn't see it happening.

"If you think he was only being nice, you're wrong," Mom said. "He wanted to know all about Parkview and the village. He had an interest in architecture and wanted to visit England to see castles and cathedrals and country estates."

"He was an architect?" The man named Nick seemed a little young to be in that profession.

"No. He was an architecture student."

"Why do you think he showed up here on the same day you arrived? You didn't give him your travel dates did you?"

She looked away and reached for the dress. "Um...no. I don't think so."

"You did. You told him."

"No, I did not." She moved to the wardrobe. With her back to me, she said, "Not in exact words, but...he may have...been able to work it out. I might have mentioned the date in September."

"I can't believe that you told a stranger so many personal details. He could have broken into your condo while you were gone."

She took the dress off the hanger, then slammed the hanger onto the rod in the wardrobe. "But he didn't. He came here and got murdered." She turned, and her eyes were glassy. "And now it's all a horrible mess with the police..."

She jerked a tissue out of the box on the dressing table and dabbed at her eyes. I wasn't big on hugging and neither was my mom. In fact, we'd probably both had so many hugs in the last few days that we'd be good for months, so I went across the room and patted her shoulder. She put her hand on top of mine for a moment then nodded briskly. "I'm fine."

"Let's concentrate on what's important," I said, mentally trying to let go of the questions and worries her actions brought to mind—was my mother routinely meeting strangers for coffee and spilling the details of her life? "Why do you think Nick came to England on the same day as you?"

"I suppose it was to see those things he mentioned...the buildings," she said, but she didn't sound convinced. "What else could it be?"

"But why would he arrive on the same day?"

"It was just one of those things. Happenstance."

I knew the police wouldn't agree, but I pressed on to the more important topic. "What did he say to you at the airport?"

She moved away and shook out the dress. "He wanted an invitation to the wedding."

"What?"

"It's true."

"But why?"

"I don't know. I didn't stop to think why or to question him about it. I told him I didn't think it would be possible."

"You did?" I asked, surprised. Usually my mom was a more-the-merrier type of person.

She fiddled with the zipper on the dress. "Yes. Normally—I would have asked you and not thought a thing about it, but..."

Her next words came out in a rush. "I didn't think it would look good."

"Why not?"

"He was young. *So* much younger than me. I wouldn't want anyone to think—it would have looked absurd, especially if he attached himself to me during the reception. I didn't want to embarrass you." She waved her hand around the room. "It's such an imposing setting with all these grand people. I didn't want anyone to think—and you...occasionally cringe at things I say and do, so I—"

"Oh, Mom—"

"You do," she said quickly.

"Okay. That's true. But you cringe at things I say and do, too. Our personalities are very different, but I'm so happy you came for the wedding." She smiled at me, and I smiled back. Her eyes looked a bit glittery, so I said, "And if you wanted to bring your boy toy, it would have been fine."

She swatted the dress at me, but I was glad to see her eyes crinkle with laughter. "I'd better change. And I'll contact that police person—the inspector—and tell him all about Nick before I go down to dinner. Give me his phone number. Interesting that you have his contact information—I want to talk to you about that later. I'll make sure he understands that it was nothing more than a few casual meetings in California and that I have no idea why Nick was here." She shooed me toward the door. "We'll let the police work out the reason he was here. That's their job after all," she said as she firmly closed me out of her room and locked the door.

CHAPTER 9

"My mom thinks I should leave everything to the police and let them sort it out," I said as Marie, our waitress, approached to remove our dinner plates.

Alex snorted and waited until she had cleared the table before he said, "Doesn't your mother know that you're not one to sit back and wait?"

"She knows it. It was her way of telling me to back off."

We were among the last guests in the Old Nether Woodsmoor Inn dining room. After I left Mom, I'd found Dad and Alex wrapping up their billiard game. Alex and I had left Parkview, intending to return to the cottage and head out again for dinner since the only food in Cart Cottage consisted of one leftover scone, but we'd gotten…distracted. We hadn't actually made it to the restaurant until much later.

I glanced around the inn's dining room with its linen tablecloths and soft candlelight. "Let's not talk about that right now." I wanted to enjoy the moment without thinking about murder or the nagging feeling of worry that I couldn't quite escape when I thought about my mom.

"Sounds good to me," Alex said as Marie returned with two cups of coffee and a plate with a slab of the inn's chocolate cake.

Alex said, "We didn't order dessert." In fact, we'd already paid for dinner.

Marie smiled, accentuating the dimples in her round face. "Tara says it's on the house. An extra wedding present. She says the ceremony was the loveliest she's seen in years."

"That's sweet of her." I drew the plate closer.

Marie added, "Even Doug said it was 'right nice,' and that's saying a lot, seeing as it was Doug who said it." Doug and Tara owned the Old Nether Woodsmoor Inn. They were the first people I'd met in the village and had been at the top of my invitation list. Doug had a build like a bulldog and manned guest check-in and the inn's office. Tara was an excellent cook whose delicious food drew people from neighboring villages to the inn's restaurant. She was a quiet and efficient sort of person, who worked in the background. Since their son had gone away to university they'd hired Marie, a local girl of about sixteen, to help with the rooms in the afternoon and with serving in the restaurant in the evening. Tara, who was checking on another table, caught Marie's eye and nodded toward another table. Marie said quickly, "Let me know if you need anything else."

Tara, a tray of cleared dishes in one hand, stopped by. "Sorry. Marie is a bit of a chatterbox."

"It's okay," I said. "Thanks for the cake."

"You're welcome. Thanks for the invitation to the wedding. We enjoyed it."

After she left, I slid my fork under a piece of cake with a thick layer of icing. "I may need a workout in the morning after this cake."

"We can do that," Alex said, and gave me a significant look.

Before I could reply, Doug approached the table, hesitated then said, "Kate...your mum—well, it seems she's trying to break into one of the guest rooms upstairs."

~

As I hurried down the low-ceilinged hall, I suppressed a groan. My mom was indeed crouched down near the handle of one of the doors at the far end of the hall. She'd changed out of the leopard print dress into a rough-weave gold sweater and jeans. The aged floorboards creaked as I picked up my pace until I was almost jogging. I heard Alex come up the stairs behind me more slowly, but I didn't wait for him. I wanted to get this sorted out before something embarrassing happened—as if having a good friend tell you your mother was having a little spot of breaking and entering wasn't embarrassing enough.

"Mom," I whispered. "What do you think you're doing?"

She jumped and dropped a thin wire. "Shush." She picked up what I now could see was an unfolded paper clip. She inserted it in the door's keyhole and jiggled it. "You'll attract attention if you don't keep your voice down." Her voice was barely audible.

"You already have. The owner of the inn came to get me from the dining room where Alex and I were having a nice dinner to tell me my mother was breaking into a room. What are you doing?"

She shook her head and continued to wiggle the paper clip in the lock. She had a second one already positioned in the lock and held it steady as she moved the first paper clip. "I'm picking this lock, dear. If you'd stop talking I might be able to get it done."

"Why?" I glanced over my shoulder, but only Alex stood in the hallway. I guessed Doug had decided to let Alex and me handle this...whatever it was.

"Because this is Nick's room, and he—er—has something of mine. I must get it back."

"I knew it. I knew you hadn't told me everything."

"Hush. I'll explain later, if you'll be quiet and let me focus. I'm sure I can do this. The people on the video on the Internet said there was nothing to it."

"You're watching lock-picking videos online? And you expect to be able to—"

The lock clicked, and my mother gave me a triumphant smile. She turned the antique handle and the door swung open.

Mom shot up and into the room. "This can't be right. He said it was room seven. This has to be it." Her gaze ran over the neatly made bed, the empty suitcase rack, and then back to the room number. "I know he said it was seven, that night at the pub. Room *seven*," she repeated, lines deepening across her forehead as she frowned.

The scent of cleaning supplies and fresh linen lingered in the air. "The police must have cleared out Nick's things, and then Tara had the room prepared for the next guest. Wait, what did you say about the pub?" I asked as she moved into the room. "Mom, stop. Was Nick at the pub?"

She jerked the doors of the wardrobe wide then scurried across the room to the small writing desk and yanked open the single drawer. "Empty," she said in a devastated tone. "It must be here. It *has* to be." She checked the small bedside table, then got down on her knees and flipped back the chintz bed ruffle. She sat up and leaned against the bed, her face pale.

I sat down beside her. The last time I'd seen that frightened look was years ago when she told me about the divorce. "Mom, what's wrong?" I asked quietly.

"You're right." The energy seemed to have drained out of her, and she spoke in a weary tone. "You always are. So clever. So smart. You'd never get yourself into something like this." She waved her hand in a circle around the room. I glanced up and saw Alex leaning against the doorframe. He gave me an encouraging smile, which my mom caught. "See, he is a keeper. Having a batty mother-in-law doesn't faze him."

"Yes, he's a catch." I sent him a smile before turning back to Mom. "Won't you tell us what this is about? Maybe we can help. I've gotten myself into some pretty tight scrapes. I didn't tell you about them because I didn't want you to worry, but I do know what it feels like when everything literally falls apart."

She frowned. "Sounds like something I should have been told about, and I want all the details—later. Right now, I suppose I better tell you about Nick."

"The whole story, this time," I said.

"Yes." She sighed. "The whole story." She shifted so that she was leaning more comfortably against the bed. "What I told you this afternoon was true. I contacted Nick about my family tree research. We met a few times, and he seemed so *nice*. I had no idea..." She paused and shook her head. "But it must have been an act. Once he found out what I'd written..."

I glanced at Alex with a frown. He closed the door and stepped into the room. "I don't understand. What had you written?"

Her shoulders relaxed at his nonjudgmental tone. "Things I'd written in my journal."

"You keep a journal?" I asked.

"Self-reflection is very important," she said, and I was glad to see some of her usual spirit return. "I've done it a while now, in fact. Every morning over coffee, I jot down a few things. And I'm completely honest about everything. It's no use to lie to yourself, is it?" She went on without waiting for an answer. "So my journals are—precious to me, that's the only way to describe them. I'd *never* forget my journal, but after I got back from coffee one morning a few weeks ago, I couldn't find it."

"You took it to the coffee shop with you?" I asked.

"Yes, of course. That's where I have my morning coffee, but when I got home it wasn't in my purse. At first I thought it had fallen out in the car. Or maybe I'd taken it out of my purse when I got home, and I'd forgotten doing that, but it wasn't anywhere—not in the car, the condo, or even in the Lost and Found at the coffee shop." She batted at the chintz ruffle, her voice tight. "Nick had it. He must have been watching me. He knew where I went to coffee, and he knew about my journal. Once, when we were meeting, he was late. I was writing in my journal when he arrived, and he asked me about it." She shook her head and sighed. "I should have put it together, but I didn't. Not until that night at the pub."

"Nick *was* at the pub?" I asked.

"Yes, for a few minutes. He insisted he had to talk to me—just like he had at the airport—and I told him I'd speak to him outside. He'd asked at the airport if I could get him into the wedding," she explained to Alex. "I thought he was going to ask again, but I hadn't changed my mind. I wasn't going to ask you for an invitation for him," she said. "But at the pub Nick said he'd already sent a message to Calista Drappell, and told her what I'd written about her in my journal. If I didn't get him into the wedding, he'd keep sending messages to other people I'd written about. He was even sending photos of my journal pages to prove what he said was true."

She sat up a bit straighter as she intercepted a glance between Alex and me. "I know it all sounds terribly juvenile and not even worth worrying about, but I spent half an hour—at international rates, at that—on the phone with Calista the next day, convincing her that I *don't* think she's a sulky cow and that the horrible shade of dark mustard that she picked out for the entrance hallway was actually very nice. It was blackmail, that's what it was. He wanted a wedding invitation and was going to keep contacting people and embarrassing me until he got what he wanted."

I said to Alex, "Calista is the president of the condo board."

Mom said, "And she does have horrible taste, but I *do* want to keep my covered parking slot."

"Calista has the power to grant parking privileges," I explained to Alex.

"And take them away," Mom added, her voice bleak.

"I'm sure it was upsetting, but I don't see—"

"How it could matter? But you were the one who told me

the police would look at me differently, now that I'd lied to them. If they found my journal—and it had my name and phone number in it...lots of numbers, actually, I was always jotting down phone numbers in it. That's how Nick found Calista's number," she said, then her voice intensified. "Don't you see? If they found my journal, they'd know that I knew Nick. I thought if I could slip in here and get it back, then they'd never need to know." Her shoulders sloped. "But it's too late for that."

"Yes, it is," I agreed, realizing that Mom's earlier assurances that she would call Quimby were a bluff. I should have known. She gave in too easily. I put those thoughts aside and focused on what Mom had just told me. "Okay, so Nick had your journal. That's not great, but other than the meetings, you had no connection with Nick, right?"

"Yes, exactly. I barely knew him. I only spoke to him a few times in California and then twice here. Once at the airport and later at the pub. If your father hadn't interfered, I could have handled it."

"Dad got involved...? Oh, Dad didn't fall, did he?"

"No. I suppose he was trying to be gallant or something like that, but I had it well in hand. I'd told Nick I'd see to an invitation, but I wanted the journal back. He agreed and said I'd get it back after the wedding, but then your father blundered in. He was so pushy. I can't say I blame Nick for giving him a good shove. I often wanted to do it myself when we were married."

I went through my memory of that night. "The man running away. He wasn't a jogger. That was Nick."

"I suppose so. He left as soon as people came out of the pub. And then you were asking all those questions and accusing me of knocking down your father. I wasn't watching so I don't know when Nick left. All I know is that I looked around before we went back in the pub, and Nick was gone."

"Sorry to accuse you of pushing Dad." I felt a bit contrite. "I should have known you wouldn't do something like that—at least not at a pub in full view of the wedding party," I added.

She cocked an eyebrow, but gave me a faint smile.

Alex asked, "So you did get this Nick guy an invitation?"

"Yes, to the reception only. He was okay with that. I asked that nice assistant, Ella. I told her I didn't want to bother either of you, and she said it wasn't a problem at all, that she'd have the invitation sent here, to room seven, which is where Nick told me he was staying when he demanded an invitation. He gave me a piece of paper with his name on it—horrible penmanship, I could barely read it—and said, 'Send it to room seven at the inn, that's where you'll find me.'" She sighed again. Mom was a master at sighing. She could convey disappointment, exasperation, and irritation, all with a puff of air. This sigh indicated she was resigned to the fact that the journal was gone. "It's too bad that I'm too late to get the journal back. As you said, the police must have it."

"Maybe not. Nick might not have brought it with him," I said.

"But that would mean he lied to me when he said I'd get it back after the wedding," Mom said. "That would be...just...wrong."

"It doesn't sound like he was worried about your good opinion," I said. "He blackmailed you."

"I suppose you're right," Mom said. "You mean he could have left it in California?"

"If he had pictures—images of the pages—why would he need to bring it? It would be another extra thing to lug around," I said. "I know that when I travel I want to take as little as possible."

"But you take the phrase 'packing light' to an absurd level," Mom said. "One suitcase. It's unnatural. Most people don't travel that way."

"But most guys have a tendency to pack lighter than women." I stood and held out a hand to Mom. "I think there might be a way to find out if Nick Davis packed light or not."

~

While Alex and my mom collected our jackets from Doug in the entryway, I returned to the inn's empty dining room. As soon as she saw me, Marie picked up a small to-go container and came across the room. "I boxed your cake for you after you and Alex disappeared. Did you want to take it with you?"

"Thanks," I said. "I'll never turn down cake." I took the box. "I suppose it's been crazy today with the police and all." I hoped I'd guessed right and that the police actually had been here. I'd assumed that because I'd heard Quimby instruct his people to begin searching the local inns that they'd found Nick's belongings and taken them. But I could be wrong. Nick could have checked out before the wedding.

"It was insane," she said. "They were in and out all afternoon." She crossed her arms and leaned against the back of a chair, settling in for a chat.

Glad that I'd guessed correctly, I said, "I suppose you saw the guy they were interested in?"

"No, he checked in on Friday afternoon and went out right away. Adventurous sort. Hiking, that sort of thing."

"How could you tell, if you didn't see him? Did Doug book him a hiking tour or something?" The countryside around Nether Woodsmoor was famous for its beauty and attracted all sorts of outdoor enthusiasts. The most frequent visitors were into cycling. The rolling terrain was ideal for biking, but walking tours were also popular. The wedding had been Saturday afternoon so Nick could have hiked on Friday afternoon or Saturday morning.

"No. I saw his stuff. Trainers, hiking boots, and knapsack— that kind of thing." She leaned in. "I saw practically *all* of his stuff. He was a messy one. Clothes and maps and books and shoes all over the place. I thought it would look worse after the police

86

searched it, but it actually looked neater. They must have straightened as they looked everything over. Probably had to."

Marie finally paused, and I managed to get a word in. "Did you happen to notice a book with a red leather cover and a black binding on the spine?" I'd asked my mom to describe her journal before we came downstairs. I was glad it had a distinctive look to it. It sounded like it would stand out, even in the clutter of Nick's room.

"No, I don't remember anything like that. It might have been there, but honestly, after I saw his little baggie..." she lowered her voice, "...of weed I didn't notice much else."

"He had drugs?"

"Not so loud." Marie looked across the empty dining room to the kitchen door. "I didn't tell Tara about it."

"And you don't want her to know now?"

"No, in case I should have reported it to her...or something. I've never come across anything like that before. I wasn't sure what to do. I let it alone and pretended I didn't see it. But maybe I should have told Tara or Doug?"

"I don't know. Ask Tara about it. I'm sure she's had the situation come up before."

"And now the police have it. They took every last thing," Marie said. "There was hardly anything left to clean in the room, only the fingerprint dust. I'm so glad I didn't touch the bag."

"Are you sure that's what it was? Maybe it was something else."

She gave me a look that I knew I'd given my mom many times when I was a teen. "I could see the bits and pieces of green leaves." The words, *Wow, Kate, you're so out of it*, were left unspoken, but I knew that's exactly what she was thinking.

I encouraged her to talk to Tara about the whole thing and said good night. Alex and Mom were waiting for me in the entryway beside Doug's reception desk. He was on the phone and gave me a nod as I joined them.

I kept my voice low. "The maid doesn't remember seeing the journal, but she says Nick's room was messy, and she might have missed it."

"That's disappointing," Mom said. "But thank you for trying to find out. I suppose I'll have to hope for the best." A car horn tooted. "That must be my ride." She looked out one of the small windows. I saw Parkview's old Range Rover idling in the parking area at the edge of the inn's courtyard.

"You had someone from Parkview drop you off for your evening of breaking and entering?" I asked.

"Of course. You didn't think I walked here, did you?"

As the car pulled away, I shook my head. "That's my mom in a nutshell, chauffeured criminal activities."

Alex and I had driven to the inn as well, and my phone rang as we left. The display showed a number I didn't recognize. I almost sent it to voicemail, but then decided I should answer.

"Kate, do you know where your mother is?"

"Dad? I didn't recognize your number."

"New phone. Is your mother with you?"

"Not at the moment." I could hear the strain in his voice. "She's on her way back to Parkview. Is something wrong?"

"The police are here and want to speak with her."

CHAPTER 10

$\mathcal{W}$hen Alex and I arrived at Parkview, the gates were open, but the bar at the ticket kiosk was down and it was closed. "I'll call Ella." She didn't live at Parkview, but she would know who to call to get us on the grounds.

"If she doesn't answer we can park here and walk in," Alex said. The thick belt of oaks that edged the road made it impossible to drive around the bar. "Or we could double back, park on the side of the road down near the maze, and walk in." Parkview's grounds were vast and, while the spacious area around the house and gardens were enclosed with a wall, the rest of the land was open. "Do you remember that path near the river that we used when we were filming that time?" Alex asked.

I nodded and was about to suggest we park where we were and walk in when Ella answered. "Ella, it's Kate. My mom is in a bit of a scrape. Alex and I need to get inside Parkview."

"I'll call Harris. He can meet you at the ticket kiosk. Use the door at the back of the west wing," she said, and gave me a code, which I repeated to Alex. He scribbled it down on one of the pads of sticky notes that he kept in the car.

By the time Harris drove out to meet us, let us inside the gate, and we drove through the grove of oaks to the house, at least twenty minutes had gone by. My phone buzzed with a text as Alex and I strode down the dim hallway. It was from Dad. "They're in the library," I said to Alex as I read the text.

The door to the estate office was closed and the rest of the hallway was in shadows. I felt as if we were in a museum after hours as we passed oil paintings, tapestries, and glass cases displaying china and porcelain. Once we reached the center block of the house, we dashed across the checkerboard floor of the entry hall to the closed door of the library. I tapped, then opened the door.

This time Quimby was seated on an armchair near the windows. My mother perched on a sofa with scroll armrests. He looked up as we entered. "Mrs.—ah—Norcutt...and Mr. Norcutt as well. I'm afraid you'll need to wait out—"

"Oh, please let them stay," Mom said.

"I've already made one exception." Quimby looked across the room.

Dad stood in a corner, hands in his pockets, his head tilted back as he squinted at the top bookshelves that ran from floor to ceiling. He didn't take his gaze off the books. "Just trying to stay out of your way."

"It's perfectly fine with me if Kate and Alex remain," Mom said as if we were about to join them for tea. "They already know about the journal, and Kate was the one who kept telling me I should call you about it." She sent Quimby a look that could only be described as coy.

Quimby's face remained as impassive as one of the Easter Island heads. Mom cleared her throat and turned the flirting down a notch. "I'd feel so much better with my daughter here, Officer."

"DCI," I corrected quietly. "His title is Detective Chief Inspector Quimby."

DEATH AT AN ENGLISH WEDDING

"Of course, that's right. Inspector Quimby, you'll let Kate and Alex stay, won't you? I would feel so much more comfortable. Not being from here, I feel at a bit of a disadvantage, you know. Since Kate has lived in England, it would be nice if she could—"

"Fine." Quimby waved us into the room. "It will actually save me time to talk with you all at the same time." I moved to the sofa and sat down beside Mom before Quimby changed his mind. Alex folded his lanky limbs into the chair opposite Quimby. A red leather book with a black binding rested on the low table in front of the sofa. It was inside a sealed plastic evidence bag.

"Since we've established that you did know Nick Davis and had quite a bit of communication with him in the States, let's go back to your meeting at the airport." Quimby consulted the screen of his phone. "What did you and Nick Davis discuss at that time?"

"I wouldn't call it a discussion," Mom said. "Nick wanted an invitation to the wedding, and I told him it wasn't possible. It was too late." Mom sent me a warning look, letting me know she didn't want to go into the original reason she'd declined to help Nick. She didn't have to warn me off. I knew I was there on sufferance, and I was going to say as little as possible. Mom turned back to Quimby. "Then Kate arrived to pick me up, and we left."

Quimby looked at me. "Did you speak to him?"

"No. As soon as Mom saw me, she left him in the coffee shop area and came over to me."

Quimby looked back to Mom. "And you saw him again...?"

Mom said, "He showed up in the pub. I couldn't believe it."

"Couldn't believe what?"

"He'd obviously followed me to Nether Woodsmoor. The nerve! He was inside the pub. It was so crowded that I didn't see him when we came inside, but he was waiting for me when I came out of the restroom. He said he had to talk to me privately. He said I'd want to hear what he had to say." She shifted position slightly. "The way he said it—well, it worried me. He seemed different, too, more...I don't know...intense. He'd always been *so* nice before. Even at the airport he had been insistent, but not rude."

"What happened next?" Quimby asked.

"I told Nick to meet me outside in front of the pub. The pub was packed with wedding guests, and I didn't want to speak to him there. When I got outside he told me about the journal, but you already know about all that," Mom said with a note of finality in her tone. "It's late. I think I'll—"

"Not yet, Mrs. Sharp," Quimby said. Mom was already standing, but sat back down quickly.

Quimby scrolled back through his notes then said, "We've been over how you agreed to get Nick Davis an invitation to the reception and arranged that through Ella Tewkesbury."

"To the reception only," Mom said. "Yes, I could see he was going to continue to make trouble, so I said I'd do it."

"Why did he want to go to the wedding reception?"

"I have no idea. He was an architecture student. I suppose that was it."

I thought of the baggie Marie had described and wondered if I should mention it. Could being under the influence of drugs explain some of Nick's behavior? But Quimby had all of Nick's possessions. If he didn't know about the drugs now, he would soon. I doubted Nick had managed to erase every trace of marijuana from his clothes and belongings.

Quimby looked up from his phone and fixed his intense green gaze, which was such a contrast to the rest of his bland appearance, on Mom. "He wasn't a student."

"Yes, he was," Mom said. "He was studying at one of the state universities—I forget which one, but I'm sure you can find out."

"No, he was between jobs." Quimby consulted another screen on his phone and read from it. "Deceased was currently unemployed. Once we identified that he was registered at the inn, we were able to use his passport to get in touch with American authorities. Nick Davis worked as a bike messenger and occasionally drove for Uber, but other than that, he didn't work. He lived with his girlfriend, who is employed as a paralegal."

Mom sucked in a breath. "But he talked about his classes and the campus and how hard he had to study."

"He lied to you," Quimby said.

"Well, I never—"

Quimby asked, "At what point did Mr. Sharp arrive outside the pub?"

"Oliver, you mean? I don't know," Mom said. "I didn't see him come outside. He appeared there and told Nick to go away."

"What exactly did he say?"

"I don't remember."

"I told him to shove off." Dad came to stand beside me at the end of the sofa. "I saw the kid and Ava through the window of the pub, and I could tell he was bothering her. I went outside and told him to leave."

Quimby turned his attention to Dad. "And then what happened?"

"He said he had every right to be there. Then he pushed me. I was on a patch of uneven ground, and I fell. The troublemaker took off before I could get to my feet."

"And a good thing, too," Mom said. "You would have only caused *more* problems. I don't know why you came outside in the first place—"

"Because I don't like to see a man bothering a woman," Dad said.

"Getting back to the point at hand..." Quimby said over both of my parents, and they subsided. "Mrs. Sharp, what did you say to Nick Davis when you met him at the reception?"

"Nothing. I didn't meet him. I stayed away from him."

"You're sure?"

"Yes. Of course."

"Mr. Sharp?"

"If you're asking if I talked to him, no, I did not," Dad said. "I didn't even know he was there."

Quimby transferred his gaze to Alex and me. "We didn't talk to him either," I said.

"That's right," Alex said. "I never saw the man."

Quimby nodded and tapped out a note on his phone, then turned back to Mom. "What did you wear to the wedding, Mrs. Sharp?"

She stared at him. "I wouldn't have thought you'd be interested in fashion." When he didn't reply, she said, "A light blue tea length dress and a matching jacket with three-quarter length sleeves. Why?"

"And a hat?"

"Of course."

"Describe it, please."

"It was wide-brimmed and made of straw, I believe. Isn't that what the salesgirl said, Kate?"

I agreed, and Quimby said, "Color?"

"The same shade of blue as my dress. We were so lucky to find something to match—"

"Lace? Feathers? Ribbon?" Quimby asked.

Mom blinked. "Yes, matching feathers and ribbon as well as some gauzy material. What is it called, Kate?"

"Tulle." I didn't like where the questions were going. My stomach suddenly felt queasy.

"That was it," Mom said.

"So this is from your hat then." Quimby removed a plastic envelope from his pocket. He held it up so that we could all see the light blue feather inside it.

Mom reached for the bag. "Yes, it is." She held it out to me.

"It's fuzzy and long, but with that sort of notched pattern cut into it."

Quimby said, "If you didn't speak to Nick Davis at the reception, how did a feather from your hat come to be found on his body in the maze?"

CHAPTER 11

"*I* don't know." Mom shoved the plastic envelope back at him.

"You're sure you didn't speak to Nick Davis yesterday?" Quimby asked, his bright green gaze fixed on Mom's face as he fingered the bag with the feather.

"Yes. Absolutely sure. I didn't talk to him or go near him." She pointed at the feather. "That must have fallen off my hat and been tracked outside...or something."

"All the way through the garden, around the lake, and into the heart of the maze?" Quimby asked.

Dad stepped forward. "Are you accusing her of murdering that man?"

"No. I'm asking questions. It's a curious thing when a bright blue feather turns up under the lapel of a dead man's suit jacket. I have to find out how it got there."

~

"Just checking on you to make sure you were able to get into Parkview and that everything is okay," Ella said.

I pressed my phone to my ear and watched the headlights cut through the darkness as Alex and I left Parkview. "Yes, we got to the house fine," I said to Ella. "But things aren't going so well, actually. Quimby was there interviewing my parents about Nick Davis."

After Quimby said he didn't have any more questions—"at this time," he'd emphasized, Mom had quickly disappeared, claiming she felt one of her migraines coming on, and Dad had patted me on the shoulder. "It will all work out, I'm sure." I didn't share his confidence.

Ella's tone shifted from professional inquiry to sympathy. "Oh, Kate. I'm sorry this is lousing up your honeymoon. DCI Quimby came and talked to me today, too. I thought that whole thing was cleared up."

"It doesn't seem to be, but you probably know more than I do," I said, thinking of her boyfriend Lucas who was a constable in another village.

"Um—I mean, that's what I heard," Ella said. "About it being nearly wrapped up."

"Really?" I asked.

"Yes."

I waited and after few seconds, she said, "Okay, I don't suppose it will hurt to tell you. Everyone in Hedgely knows it anyway. Lucas wouldn't have told me otherwise."

"I won't say anything, except to Alex, of course."

"I'd expect nothing less from newlyweds." I could hear the smile in her voice.

"I'm putting you on speakerphone then," I said.

"Okay. Well, it's not much. Remember the woman at the wedding who made a fuss in the back corner of the room? Did you notice her?"

"Yes. She had long dark hair and was dressed in a jean jacket."

Alex raised his eyebrows. "You noticed that from across the room?"

"She stood out. Everyone else was dressy," I said to Alex, then angled the phone closer to me as I said to Ella, "You hustled her out quickly."

"I happened to be on that side of the room and was able to get her out before she made a scene. I couldn't understand everything she said, but I did catch few words. She was saying, 'I knew it. I knew there was someone else.' She was trembling and near tears. I got her out of there and calmed her down, but she wouldn't say anything else. I told her she had to leave Parkview, that the wedding was a private event. I thought she might argue, but she went without a murmur. Of course, I had someone escort her off the grounds. I didn't think a thing about it until this afternoon when Lucas called and said DCI Quimby was on his way over to speak to me. They'd managed to figure out the identity of the guy who was killed."

"Nick Davis," I said.

"Yes. They'd found out he was staying in the inn and traced some of his movements. They knew he came to the reception and sat at the back. One of the waiters mentioned 'the crazy crying girl,' and since she had done her shrieking near the guy who died, they talked to Neal, who escorted her to the gates. Do you know Neal?"

"No, I don't think so." I'd met a lot of people at Parkview when we filmed there, but the estate employed too many people to know them all by name.

"You'd know him, if you'd met him. He's not one to sit in silence, even for a few minutes. Big on finding out where people are from. He usually works the entry desk. You know that map on the wall with all the pins in it?" she asked, referring to a wall-size world map with the heading "The World Visits Parkview." It bristled with push pins.

"Yes. I put a pin in southern California for me."

"Neal takes care of the map, and he's not one to let someone leave Parkview without hearing where they're from. Once he got her talking, he found out she was from California and was staying in Hedgely while she was here. After the police interviewed Neal, they tracked *her* down. She's still in Hedgely, and get this—she's Nick's fiancée. She followed him here because she was sure that he was cheating on her. Lucas interviewed the owner of the B&B where she's staying. Apparently, she tried to find a room in Nether Woodsmoor, but couldn't. Doug sent her over to Hedgely. Like I said, the word is out about her in Hedgely. She's been stroppy ever since she arrived and hasn't bothered to hide it." I detected a trace of disapproval in Ella's tone.

"Not keeping a stiff upper lip, then," I said.

"Far from it," Ella said. "No one in the police force actually came out and said that they think she…you know…did it, but she *was* engaged to him. I got the feeling that they were concentrating on her. She's their main suspect, I guess."

"Thanks for telling us, Ella." At least my parents weren't the only people Quimby was talking to. "Do you happen to know what her name is?"

"Let me think…I'm sure I heard someone—either Neal or someone else—mention it. It was a name related to plants, I remember that. Maybe Ivy or Willow? Oh, wait—Fern! That was it. Fern."

"But what do the police think happened?" Alex asked. "You said Fern was escorted off the grounds. Did she come back later? And how did she and Nick end up in the maze?"

All good questions that I hadn't thought of. I hadn't gotten past feeling relieved that the police had another suspect in view besides my mom.

"You know how wide open Parkview is," Ella said. "Fern could have come back later and parked down the road. It's not that far to walk in."

"We considered it earlier," I said more to Alex than Ella, and he nodded.

Ella must not have heard because she went on. "I have no idea

99

about how the maze fits into it. Maybe he agreed to meet her there or something. Maybe she snuck back in and followed him. Maybe he got lost again. I went back to the estate office to get a sweater after the speeches and found him wandering the halls."

"That's a long way from the conservatory," Alex said.

"Happens all the time with tourists," Ella said. "They lag behind the group and get turned around. The corridors and staircases can get pretty confusing. He said he'd left to go to the loo and taken a wrong turn." Her voice changed, becoming brisk. "But you're newlyweds. Don't worry about it. The police will sort it out. You go enjoy your honeymoon at your cute little cottage."

"Does everyone know we're staying in Cart Cottage?" I asked after I ended the call.

"Looks that way," Alex said. "Nether Woodsmoor is just like Hedgely when it comes to secrets. It's hard to keep anything quiet here."

"And yet no one seems to know what Nick was doing here, or why he wanted to go to the wedding."

CHAPTER 12

"That's a good one," Alex said.

I made a humming noise of agreement, selected the photo, and swiped to the next one. It was late Monday morning, and we were at the White Duck seated at a tall round table, studying my phone. Louise's newest hire, Shannon, had already whisked away our empty breakfast plates, but we were lingering over our coffee. Normally, the pub was only open in the afternoon, but Louise had been experimenting with opening for breakfast during Nether Woodsmoor's busiest season. Now that it was September, things were slowing down. Parkview was now only open for weekend tours, and I supposed by the time we returned from our honeymoon—if we got to go—Louise would have switched back to normal hours at the pub. I'd have to go back to making my second cup of coffee myself.

"Really like the giraffe in that one," Alex said.

"Um-hmm." I selected the photo and swiped to the next one. "Wait." I went back to the photo. "Did you say giraffe?"

"Just checking to see if you're paying attention."

I put my phone down and reached for my coffee. "Sorry." I shook my head. "I can't concentrate on wedding photos this morning." The photographer had sent the digital proofs, but I was having a hard time narrowing down the images from the hundreds she'd sent.

Last night, we'd picked up Chinese food then gone back to Cart Cottage where we'd eaten in front of the fire. Ella's phone call had given me some reassurance that the police would arrest Nick's murderer soon—and it wouldn't involve my mother—so I was able to put the whole thing out of my mind and have a nice evening with Alex, but this morning all my worries had returned. "I keep wondering what Quimby is doing. Do you think he's made an arrest?"

Alex took a sip of his coffee. "I think we'd know if he had. It wouldn't take long for the word to get around."

"You're right."

Shannon paused at our table. "More coffee?"

"No, I'm too edgy," I said.

"So have you heard the news from Parkview?"

I sat up. "No. What?"

"They've found that guy's wallet, the dead guy's. It was blocking one of the drains from the lake—you know they use the water from the lake for the other fountains and things, right? It's incredible what they were able to do so long ago."

"Yes," I said. "We've done the tour." Parkview's water features were an intricate connected system. Water pumped from the lake, which was at a higher level, powered several of the fountains in the gardens. I knew the groundskeepers were winterizing the system and many of the fountains had already been shut down like the one at the center of the maze, but several in the gardens around the house were still working.

"They found a mobile, too. It wasn't with the wallet, but it was in the same part of the lake. Raked it right out, Gabe said. He's a groundskeeper. He stopped in here after going to the church hall to sign his statement. Whoever did in the poor murdered bloke tossed his mobile and wallet in the lake, but didn't realize it was so near one of the drains. And the wallet was full of cash and credit cards. Must have chucked it in the lake without even looking inside."

"Yes, they must have." My heart sank as the last hope of the police closing the case quickly disappeared. I'd wanted to hear through the village grapevine this morning that Nick Davis had died in a botched robbery, that Mom's journal was irrelevant, and that the feather from her hat found at the crime scene had been a bizarre coincidence. Or, that if it was murder, then the fiancée had done it and was under arrest.

Alex must have been tracking along the same distressing thoughts because he looked as somber as I felt. But Shannon had shifted to talking about Alex's greyhound, Slink, and I could tell Alex made an effort to put his worries aside and focus on what she was saying. I tried to do the same thing.

Louise and I had both taken care of Slink in the past when Alex had to go out of town, but Louise was extra busy with the longer hours at the pub. She had mentioned that Shannon was always working odd jobs to earn some more money, so we'd asked her to watch Slink. Since Alex and I had both stayed in Parkview the night before the wedding, Shannon had taken Slink home with her that day, saying she'd keep her for us until we returned from Venice. "She'll settle better if she's not going back and forth," Shannon had said, and Alex had agreed.

Shannon said, "Slink is *such* a good dog. I took her to the green last night and threw the tennis ball for her, like you said to do. I can't believe how fast she is. She's like a blur when she lets loose." I was glad to see Shannon looking so relaxed and happy. I knew that Louise had some trouble training Shannon, but hadn't wanted to let her go.

"Butterfingers," I remembered Louise had said, her tone exasperated. "She's broken three glasses and two plates, but she's got nowhere else to go, poor lamb." Louise had sighed. "Dad's done a bunk. There's some trouble there. Something shady, I think, so it's probably best he's gone, but her mom is scatty and can't seem to hold a job."

Fortunately, Shannon hadn't broken much more of "the crockery" as Louise called it, and had settled down, growing more self-assured as the days went by. She was extremely fair and had a long thin nose and small dark eyes. The fact that she parted her fine pale blond hair in the center of her head and pulled it back into a long braid only increased her resemblance to a mouse, but over the last few months she's gained confidence and looked less like a mouse hungry for a bit of cheese. Now she smiled at regular customers and easily carried trays stacked with dishes, confidently stepping through the tables.

Shannon said, "Don't worry about Slink. She's such a sweetheart. She's adjusted to my house, no problem. I love having her around. When do you leave for your trip?"

Alex and I exchanged a glance. "Tuesday afternoon," I said in a tone that masked my uncertainty about leaving Nether Woodsmoor. With the investigation going on would we even be allowed to go?

I felt a presence behind me as Shannon looked over my shoulder and said, "Oh, hello, Mr. Sharp. Can I bring you something?"

"Ah—yes. Coffee, black," Dad said in a preoccupied way then looked after Shannon as she departed.

He asked, "Does everyone in this place know who I am?"

"Pretty much," I said. "It's a small village. Visitors stand out. Shannon probably recognized you because you were in here the night before the wedding."

"Right. Right," Dad said. "Then why does no one remember that kid, Nick?" He spoke more to himself than to us.

I patted the table. "Sit down with us, Dad. What do you mean?" I asked as Alex dragged over another chair.

Dad hitched himself onto the tall chair. "I've been asking around about this Mr. Nick Davis. No one remembers him. The only person who I could actually pin down who definitely recalled talking to Nick was the squat guy who looks like a body-builder."

"That would be Doug, the owner of the inn," Alex said.

"Right. He said he remembered the young man checking into the inn, but beyond that strange haircut, he couldn't describe him. Said he saw the guy once, and only for a minute or two." Shannon brought his cup of coffee. Dad waited until she'd moved away, then he leaned over the table.

"What I want to know is why Nick Davis was keeping to himself. What was he up to?"

"Why were you asking about Nick?" I asked. I hadn't wanted to disturb Dad last night, but I probably should have called him after I talked to Ella to let him know the police had suspects other than Mom.

"The police detective, the DCI, came to see me again this morning. He wanted to know what size shoe I wear."

"That doesn't sound good," I murmured, then asked, "Did he tell you why?"

"No, but I have a pretty good idea." He took a slug of his coffee then continued. "I told him size ten, and he looked over at the guy who came with him—a junior officer of some sort. That guy looked up something online. He nodded and said, 'The converted size matches, sir.'"

"They converted your shoe size from an American measurement to a UK measurement," I said slowly, and my large breakfast suddenly wasn't settling so well. "The only reason to do that would be..."

"Because they're looking for a man who was at the crime scene," Dad finished, his tone grim. "And if the look those two men exchanged this morning means what I think it means...then they're pretty sure they found the guy." He pointed his thumb at his chest. "Me. They think it was me."

"But that's—crazy. Why would they think that?" I asked.

"Because they think your mother was there," Dad said. "I've already admitted that I butted in when the guy was giving her problems the night before the wedding. I'm the first person they think of when they ask themselves who would help your mother."

I rubbed my temples. "You're saying that the police are trying to link *both* of you to the murder?"

"They're operating on the assumption that your mother was out there at the Greek temple thing with Nick Davis. I'm sure their thinking runs something like this: Ava is traveling in a foreign country and runs into trouble. Who is she going to ask for help? Not her daughter, the bride. And not her new son-in-law either. Especially not on their wedding night. No, she'd go to the one person she could. She'd hate to ask anything of me, but if she had no one else...well, it wouldn't matter would it? She'd come to me."

"On second thought, I think I need more coffee." I signaled Shannon. "Did you say something about the folly? That's not where the body was found."

"No, but I think that's where the murder happened. I went out there this morning after the DCI left. He took my shoes with him, by the way. I took a look around the maze and the folly, as you called it."

"Quimby took your shoes?" My stomach churned.

"Sealed up tight in an evidence bag, just like on a crime show. Now, don't look so worried, Katie. I haven't been out in the gardens or even over that hill until this morning, so once they figure that out, it will all be fine."

Dad hadn't called me Katie in years, and I knew he was trying to make me feel better, but I couldn't ignore what he'd told us. "But that could take weeks," I said. "It's not like on television when they get the results back the same day."

"Everything at the maze is cleaned up now." Dad went on with his train of thought. "The police have taken away all their crime tape, but it's obvious from the trampled grass which area they were most interested in—and that's the area around the folly. The section right around the stairs, in particular. I'm not an expert on cleaning, but even I could see that someone had given the steps on the folly a serious scrubbing. The treads are a pale white stone. One section was much lighter than the rest. I chatted with the girl who brought my coffee this morning at Parkview. She's dating one of the groundskeepers, and he said that someone had been dispatched early this morning with thick gloves and plenty of bleach to clean several drops of blood off the steps." He smiled briefly. "So I suppose this tight-knit community thing where everyone knows everyone else's business has its advantages."

"It can come in handy," Alex said.

"I found one other thing out there by the folly." He gave the word *folly* an exaggerated flourish. He took out his phone then began tapping and sliding his finger across the screen.

"A smartphone, Dad?" My dad was not a fan of innovation. I could remember him complaining about Facebook. He'd said, "Virtual friendship—what is that? I'll tell you what it is. It's an oxymoron. How can you be friends through a computer screen?"

He spoke with his attention still fixed on the screen. "I know. It's a sad sign when a Luddite like me gives in." His voice turned regretful. "I had to do it. Too much happens online now for me not to be 'connected,' as they say. But it turns out that I'm quite the social media whiz. You should check out the bookshop's Instagram feed. Oh, here it is." He turned the phone toward Alex and me. "I found that, too."

The photo was of a patch of mud with a shoe print at almost dead center. The indentation showed a separate square heel, tapered toe, and smooth tread.

CHAPTER 13

"*A* man's dress shoe?" Alex asked as he looked at the photo on my dad's phone.

"I think so," Dad said. "Most of that area around the folly is grassy, except right up against the edge of the bottom step. I think this footprint is what caused them to come look for me. I checked the rest of the ground in the area, but didn't find anything else. Grass everywhere, even in the maze. In fact, the paths of the maze have some sort of special low-growing turf that's springy and doesn't hold footprints. Even with all the tracking back and forth that the police did in the maze, the grass doesn't show a single imprint."

"No wonder they latched onto the footprint by the folly," I said. "Especially since Nick wore running shoes."

Alex said, "The tread on Nick's shoes would have left a completely different imprint."

Dad said, "Ah, so the chances are good that the footprint might belong to the murderer—someone wearing a men's dress shoe in my size."

"But that could be a huge portion of the wedding guests or

staff," I said. "Or even someone who happened to wander by earlier in the day."

"It is possible that it could be completely unrelated, but I'm sure Quimby is running through everyone's shoe size now," Alex said. "Did you find out anything else?"

"Only that a steak knife went missing from the kitchen. They were one short when they cleaned up after the wedding. I discovered that from another of Parkview's staff this morning before I walked here. I've noticed lots of the Brits are a bit standoffish, but not this guy. He wanted to know where I was from and what it was like in Kansas."

"Must have been Neal," I said.

"That was his name. He told me about the map with visitors' hometowns. Since he was asking questions, I asked a few of my own. He said the chatter with the staff is about that missing steak knife. Still hasn't turned up, but he's sure that was what was used to kill Nick."

"It could be. I did notice the knife when we were in the maze," I said. "In fact, I was sort of mesmerized by it. It had a slender silver handle like the cutlery used at the reception. I wanted to look away, but couldn't seem to make myself do it. It was such a strange thing to see, and there was so little blood."

"If the knife is left in the body, there can be only a small amount of bleeding," Dad said. "Some, but not a lot."

"Don't let Quimby here you saying things like that," I said.

"It's common knowledge to any mystery reader."

I'd inherited my love of mysteries from my dad but didn't want him broadcasting his specialized knowledge, especially when it seemed Quimby was so interested in him. "Still, probably best to keep it to yourself," I said. "Neal could be right, that someone picked up a knife during the reception and used it later to kill Nick." I handed the phone back to Dad. "This is not good. If that's what happened, then it's something else that ties Nick to our wedding." The list of links to the wedding was growing—the menu card, Mom's feather, and now possibly the knife.

"Not necessarily," Alex said. "It could be that the knife was misplaced and will turn up later."

Dad said, "I plan to chat with everyone I come across today about the incident. I figure they'll speak freely—at least until the word spreads that the police think that your mom and I were in it together."

"But that makes no sense at all," I protested. "Why would you or Mom—either together or separately—want to kill Nick? You have no motive."

Dad swept a trace of sugar off the table with his hand. "You're forgetting about your mother's blasted journal. Why Ava had to turn introspective at this point in her life is a mystery to me. And then to go and lose the thing. I'm sure the police think she killed Nick then asked me to help her move the body to the maze to keep it from being discovered right away." He broke off and took a long sip of his coffee as if to keep himself from saying more.

I said, "Mom wouldn't want her journal made public, but I don't think that it would drive her to murder someone."

"Unfortunately, it sounds as if that journal—and the fact that Nick was using it to blackmail your mom—is all the police have now as far as a motive," Alex said.

"Then we have to find something else." The butterflies in my stomach settled down. Alex drew a breath, and I added, "You know I feel better when I'm doing something. I can't sit around and—pick out wedding pictures and pack for our trip to Venice when I don't know if we'll even be able to get on the plane."

Alex gave me a long look over his coffee cup. "You are a take-charge person, I do agree with that."

I said, "We're only expediting things for the police. They'll eventually come to the conclusion that Mom and Dad had nothing to do with Nick's death, but it may take them days or even weeks to discover definite evidence that clears them. If we talk to a few people maybe we can shake out a few other suspects for Quimby to look at. You know he's thorough. If we bring him evidence that someone else could be involved, he'll check it out." I put my hand over Alex's. "I have a feeling that if we don't give the investigation a nudge, we might be stuck here for quite a while."

Alex turned his hand and laced his fingers through mine. "I can't argue with that."

Dad cleared his throat. "You're sharp, Alex. It took me a long time to realize that when Kate decides to get something done, it's best to get on board or get out of the way."

"That makes me sound so bossy."

"You are," Dad said with a grin.

"But only about the things that you are passionate about—the things you love," Alex added.

"I think you two are getting along a little too well." I surveyed them both with mock severity, then said, "Okay, so where were we?"

"Your mother and her journal and Nick's blackmailing her about it," Dad said. "Weak motive."

"I agree." I sat up straight. "I know that Mom has her moments, but she wouldn't stab someone any more than she'd...I don't know...bake a cake from scratch."

Dad chuckled. "Still the queen of the to-go order, is she?"

"Always," I said. To Alex, I added, "Thank goodness you know your way around the kitchen."

Alex shrugged. "I know a little."

"You can make more than a grilled cheese sandwich and omelets, so you're miles ahead of me." I turned back to Dad and asked, "Where is Mom?"

"Migraine."

"That's too bad." Mom had a terrible time with migraines. She hadn't ever found a medicine that worked for her. She'd be in her room most of the day with the drapes closed, trying to sleep it off, which was the only thing that worked for her. "Then I doubt we'll see her until tomorrow, but there are a few things that we can do today."

I gave Alex's hand a squeeze before letting go and reaching for a paper napkin. I wished I had my Moleskine journal with me, but it was packed away. Dad took a pen from the inside pocket of his sport coat and handed it to me. Using feathery strokes, I wrote "Questions" at the top of the napkin. "These questions have been running around in my mind all morning." I jotted them down as I spoke. "I think the biggest one is why did Nick want to come to the wedding? No matter how interested you are in architecture, you don't buy an airline ticket and bribe your way into a wedding just to see the interior of a stately home."

"Especially when that stately home is open during other times of the year," Alex said. "He could have toured it anytime during the summer or waited until next weekend when it's open to visitors."

"So why did he want to get in during the wedding? To meet someone who'd be there specifically for that event?" I asked. "It couldn't have been either of us." I moved the pen back and forth between Alex and me. "Nick didn't even attempt to get near us."

"And he didn't bother your mother during the reception," Dad said. "So it must have been someone else."

"But that's rather hit or miss, isn't it?" I said. "*We* had the names of the RSVPs, but how would Nick have known who would be there? What if he hoped to meet someone there, but they didn't come? And if he did want to connect with another guest, why would he travel all the way to England just to meet someone? Wouldn't calling them be much easier?"

A silence descended for a few seconds, then I said, "Okay, we'll leave that one. Maybe we can get in touch with his fiancée, Fern. She might know something about why he came here and wanted to go to the wedding reception." I wrote "Fern" on the napkin.

"And you have to wonder what he was doing between the

time he arrived here in England and when he showed up at the pub the night before the wedding," Dad said.

"Good question." I put it down. "Where did he spend Wednesday afternoon, Thursday, and Friday morning? We know he arrived at the inn on Friday afternoon." I explained about the conversation with Marie then added, "Marie said she saw a baggie of weed in his room, which might explain some of Nick's erratic behavior." I'd already told Alex about the conversation I'd had with Marie and wanted to see what my dad made of the detail.

"Hard to say how drugs would affect a person, but doesn't seem to go with someone who travels halfway across the world and blackmails someone to get into a wedding," Dad said.

"Well, it's a question that needs to be answered." I wrote it down, then started a new column. "Here's what we do know. Nick was a blackmailer. If he used threats to get Mom to do what he wanted, he might have done it to someone else. What else do we know about him?"

"Quimby said he lived in San Bernardino," Alex said. "He worked occasionally, but didn't have a steady job."

"He was a bum, sponging off his girlfriend," Dad said. "And he was a twenty-five-year-old kid, who met your mother for coffee, and listened to her yak, probably for hours. He had to be playing some sort of long game—something shady, I bet."

I read over the list. "Blackmailer, liar, possible conman."

"Sounds like there should be plenty of people who would want to bump him off," Dad said.

I nodded. "We just have to find them."

"Oh, I thought of something else." I reached for my phone and brought up the wedding photos. "Maybe Nick is in some of the pictures from the reception." Dad and Alex looked over my shoulder as I scanned the images. We zipped through the images of the family groups, but I slowed down when we came to the candid shots of guests seated at the tables. After a few minutes, we all tensed. "That's him." I enlarged the photo as much as I could on my phone.

"Who's beside him?" Dad asked.

"That's the organist," I said, "but I don't remember her name."

"Sylvia," Alex supplied.

"That's right. We met her briefly during the reception. She wasn't with Nick then."

"She sure looks friendly with him in that picture," Dad said, and I had to agree. The photo wasn't one of those posed photos with stiff expressions that usually were the result of the photographer calling for everyone to smile. The camera had caught Nick and Sylvia sharing a glance that had an intimacy that was easy to see.

"It looks like they were getting along pretty well," Alex said. "I think we better add Sylvia to the list of people who might know something."

"Done," I said. "I'll call Ella and see if she can put us in touch with her."

Dad tapped the list. "That girlfriend of his, the one who caused the stir at the reception, she's where we should start. And you're the one who should tackle her, Kate. Girl talk and all that."

"I think you're right," I said. "But I'll bring Alex along. He's much better at sussing out emotional notes than I am."

"Good." Dad braced his hands to push back from the table. "I'll head back to Parkview and see who else I can talk to. Who knows what someone might have seen."

Alex said, "Did you have other plans for today?"

"Well, yes. I was supposed to go to Sheffield. A bookseller there says he has a first edition of *A Christmas Carol*," he said regretfully.

"I think it might be a good idea if you continued with your normal plans. See that man by the window?" Alex tilted his head slightly, indicating a burly man with cropped dark hair. He looked to be in his late twenties. A day's growth of beard gave him a dark shadow on his cheeks. A button-down shirt strained across his shoulders, and a barn jacket rested on the back of his chair. "He came in a few minutes after you did and has kept an eye on our table the whole time you've been here." A folded newspaper, the local weekly, was propped on the table in front of him.

Dad discreetly looked over his shoulder. "I think I saw him on the path on my way here."

"You walked?" I asked.

"It's not far, and it's a nice morning. The weather is supposed to turn later, so I wanted to get outside while I could. I stopped at that arched stone bridge to look at the water. That's when I saw him. He was walking slowly, doing something on his phone. In fact, that's why I noticed him. Can't imagine being so tied to your phone that you can't take your eyes off it while you walk through the countryside here."

"I think he's following you," Alex said. "I bet he's with the police."

Dad's eyebrows shot up. "Tailing me? Why would he—oh, I get it. To see if I do anything suspicious...like try to dispose of clothes with blood on the cuff or something of that sort."

"It could be a coincidence," I said. "Maybe he's enjoying his coffee and reading the paper."

"He hasn't turned the page once," Alex said.

"Oh."

"And he has a sort of contained energy about him," Alex said. "Whatever he's doing, he's not relaxing with his morning coffee." Alex leaned toward Dad. "It would probably be better if you went about your day as you originally planned. If you spend your day questioning people about the night of the reception..."

"It could look as if I'm meddling, maybe even trying to shake out someone who saw me doing something nefarious."

"Exactly," Alex said. "That's why you should go to—where was it?—Manchester?"

"Sheffield."

"Go to Sheffield, and take your watcher with you. Let him see you visit bookshops and whatever else you had planned," Alex said.

"Once Dad gets in a bookshop, good luck getting him out," I said. "Especially when it's an antique bookshop. He'll be there all day. You should certainly be able to tell if Mr. Five-O'clock Shadow is trailing you."

"And if he's not," Dad said. "I'll come back here and check in with you two—after I look at that copy of *A Christmas Carol*, of course."

"Of course." I couldn't help but smile. "It would be a shame to go all that way and then not see it. We'll go over to Hedgely and see if we can talk to Fern. I'll call you if we find out anything."

Dad checked his watch. "I think I can catch the next bus to Sheffield. I won't look back. Let me know if he follows."

"You know which bus you want?" I asked.

"Lucky number thirteen, departing from the bus stop at the village green." He stood. "I got the details this morning from that stuffy guy with the bow tie."

"Malcolm," I said.

Dad nodded. "Knows his bus routes, despite acting like he's the king of England." He raised his voice slightly as he said, "Okay, I'm off to see some books."

"Don't overdo it," I murmured in a low voice.

"Me? Never." He winked.

Alex and I stayed at the table. A few seconds after Dad left, I saw movement out of the corner of my eye at the table where the guy with the five-o'clock shadow had been seated. Alex was facing that direction. He raised his mug and said from behind it, "Mr. Five-O'clock Shadow is gone. He's keeping back about ten paces or so, but he's heading in the direction of the green."

CHAPTER 14

*H*edgely was a twenty-minute drive from Nether Woodsmoor, but the countryside had a wilder and more dramatic feel to it. The hills were higher and the drops to the streams that wound through the landscape were steeper. Rocky outcroppings of limestone thrust out of the hills, creating craggy promontories. The gray clouds sweeping in on gusts of wind added to the feeling that we were driving into a scene from a gothic novel.

"All that's missing is a castle with crumbling walls," I said, looking at the darkening sky, "and we'd have the perfect setting to film something like *The Mysteries of Udolpho*. But we'd also need the woman in a flowing white nightgown, running across the landscape."

"Goes without saying," Alex said, and we exchanged a smile, then he checked the rearview mirror, something that he'd been doing quite a bit on the drive.

"Still nothing?" I asked.

"Nope. I guess Quimby thinks we're not important enough to follow."

"You sound disappointed."

"It would be fun to try and lose someone on these twisty roads," Alex said.

"Well, I'm glad we're not under police surveillance. It looks like it's going to rain, and I wouldn't want to slide off the road into a ditch."

"Spoilsport," Alex said in a good-natured tone.

"I do wish I'd brought my camera, though," I said. "The light is so interesting." While the darker clouds and their shadows flowed overhead, in the distance the sky was still clear and bright, casting a glow that filtered under the growing cloud cover. I rarely went anywhere without my camera, but both Alex and I had decided to take a break from work during our honeymoon. I had packed my camera in my suitcase, but I only planned to take photos of the canals and palazzos in Venice—pure tourist stuff.

"That's the turn for Hedgely." I moved from thinking about the dramatic view to what I'd say to Fern. Cold-calling was nothing new to Alex or me. We'd done a lot of that sort of thing, but it was the least favorite part of my job for me.

"Any ideas on how to approach her?" I asked. Alex's excellent people instincts made him my go-to guy in situations like this. His easy-going persona disarmed people and, in most cases, they were happily chatting with him in a few minutes.

"I think you're up this time. I have a feeling she's off men right now."

"You're probably right," I said, then added, "but we have to find her first. We don't even know her last name."

"I don't think that will be a problem," Alex said. We rounded a curve in the road, and the village came into view. Tucked into a fold of one of the steep hills, Hedgely consisted of a grocery, a pub with a sign stating that rooms were available, and a smattering of houses.

"No, definitely not," I said. "In fact, I think that's her." As Alex stopped near the pub, I pointed to a figure in a puffy gray coat moving away from the tiny village. As she strode up a narrow footpath on the hill, the wind whipped her dark hair behind her. She glanced over her shoulder once, and I could make out her heavy straight brows. "Yep, that's Fern." I opened my door. "Looks like she's going out for a long walk. I'll see if I can catch up to her."

"Oh, I don't doubt you can do that. You're quite the walker," Alex said. "I'll wait for you at the pub."

I set off, buttoning my pea coat, glad for the warmth of the wool. The temperature was dropping rapidly, and I wished I'd thought to grab my gloves as well. The narrow footpath twisted up the steep incline of the hill. Fern was several yards ahead of me. I concentrated on my footing. Exploring the walking paths that crisscrossed Nether Woodsmoor and the surrounding countryside was one of my favorite things to do, but the landscape around the village was much flatter than this hike. After a few minutes, I was breathing heavily. I needed to add in a couple of walks with hills to my rambles.

I reached the summit of the hill, drew in a deep breath, and admired the view for a moment. Now that I was at the top, I could see the ridge that formed the spine of the hill was limestone. Unlike the side that sloped to Hedgely at an acute angle, the other side of the hill dropped away in a sheer cliff, straight down to a thread of silver water that sparkled in the remaining sunlight as it flowed over rocks. The incoming clouds cast a shadow over the hillside on the other side of the stream. The shadow inched down the slope toward the stream at a steady pace.

"Beautiful, isn't it?" I said to Fern who had also stopped at the top and was standing a few feet up the ridge. She didn't reply. Instead, she turned her back on me and went along the ridge to an outcropping that hung over the drop to the stream. She scrambled up the rock, then sat and let her legs dangle over the edge. The wind buffeted her face, sending her hair streaming out behind her head.

I eyed the rock and decided I wouldn't join her on the perch. I'd caught a glimpse of her face. Now that I was closer I could see that her eyes were swollen, and her nose was pink. I felt bad about chasing her up the hill. She obviously wanted to be alone, but I'd come this far...and she might be able to provide some answers that would help straighten out what had happened with Nick. "Sorry to intrude on you like this, but I'm Kate—er— Norcutt," I said, stumbling over my married name. "It was my wedding reception that Nick came to."

Her head whipped toward me, and I sucked in a breath, afraid that she'd lose her balance with the sudden movement. But she had her hands braced on the rock. "You know that slut, Ava? She's a friend of yours?"

"Ava—? You think he went to the wedding to meet Ava?" I asked.

"I know he did. I saw him beside her at the reception. He said he wasn't seeing someone else, but I *knew* he was. I knew he was lying." Anger mixed with triumph filled her tone.

"I don't doubt that he lied to you about many things, but that wasn't Ava he was sitting beside at the wedding. That was the organist, Sylvia. Ava is my mother."

"Your *mother?*"

"Yes, I promise, it's true." I explained how my mother had contacted Nick then described how he had met her several times in California.

"Your mother?" She seemed stuck on that fact, and I can't say that I blamed her. She pulled her legs back from the edge and twisted around to face me. "You're saying he *wasn't* fooling around with Ava?"

"I know he and my mother weren't...together. My mother thought he was a nice boy who was interested in genealogy. Did you know he was interested in that sort of thing? Family trees, ancestors...stuff like that?"

"No. He didn't care about anything like that."

I took a step to the rock and leaned on it. "Look, Nick obviously lied to you and to my mom. Why don't you come down and let me buy you a cup of coffee or tea or something at the pub? Maybe we can figure out what Nick was doing." The cloud's shadow had darkened the stream, blotting out the flashes of reflected sunlight that danced on the water, and was now creeping up the sheer fall of rock below us.

Her heavy brows lowered. "No. I hate that place. All everyone does is whisper about me. I can't wait to get out of here."

"Well, then, let's talk here," I said quickly. The stiff breeze was chilling my fingers and ears. I removed my hands from the cold rock and shoved them into my pockets. "Do you have any idea why Nick came to England?"

"No." I thought that was all she would tell me, but then she slid across the rock and dropped down. "There's a more sheltered place over here."

She moved away from the ridge to a section of rock that overlooked Hedgely. The outcropping of limestone rose to about eight feet overhead, but part of it had worn away creating a curved area with a little shelf of rock that protruded from the formation, creating a bench-like seat.

She plopped down and pulled her knees up to her chest. "He started acting weird this summer. His mom had passed away, and I thought he'd get back to normal soon, but he spent hours and hours clearing out her house and a storage unit she had. He wasn't a detailed person, but he was obsessive about her stuff. He had to look at each thing, read every scrap of paper...I didn't get it. I tried to cut him some slack—you know, his mom *had* just died. Anyway, it was about that time that he got all secretive. Didn't want me to read his texts, and he kept leaving the room when he got phone calls. I looked at his call log on his phone. He was calling 'Ava.' We don't have any friends named Ava. When I asked him what was going on, he said it was all part of a plan, that he'd be able to tell me about it later when we were rolling in it."

The stone bench wasn't big enough for two, so I leaned against a nearby outcropping of rock. "Money? He thought he'd come into some money?" I wondered if Nick was blackmailing someone else with much deeper pockets than my mom—maybe someone with a much bigger secret, too.

"Yeah, that's what he meant, but he'd already gotten his inheritance from his mom. I couldn't figure out what he was talking about."

"So you suspected another woman?"

"Of course. No matter what he said, his actions said he was seeing someone else. He was vague about where he was going, and then he came home a few times smelling like Miss Dior."

I knew that fruity scent. "That's what my mom wears," I said.

Fern hugged her knees tighter. "Well, I was right. He was seeing another woman, even if it was just coffee with your mom. Why would he do that? And even if he didn't come to the wedding to see your mom, I saw the way he looked at that girl beside him. He used to look at me that way." She focused on the fabric of her jeans as she blinked rapidly.

It didn't sound like she knew much about what Nick had been up to, but I didn't want her to stop talking—it might be the smallest tidbit that would unlock everything—so I said, "You followed him here. That's a...quite a big step to take."

She sniffed and seemed to get her emotions under control. "My best friend thought I was insane, but I had to know. And how else could I find out? Nick always had some reason, some excuse, for everything. I figured following him was the only way to know for sure. I saw his airline ticket was from LAX to England. He'd told me he was going to Miami. Miami! I decided that if I confronted him, he'd only lie to me again. By then I wanted to catch him out and embarrass him." She tightened her grip around her knees, drawing them closer to her chest. "I wanted to win. If I could prove he was a rat, then I'd have beaten him."

I didn't follow her logic, but I supposed that when a guy gives you the runaround, different girls react in different ways. I always cut my losses and moved on. Apparently, Fern was big on revenge. How big on revenge was the question. Was it important enough to her to kill Nick? Looking over the sniffling, pink-eyed woman in front of me, I wasn't sure that she'd killed him, but she'd certainly proved that she was dogged. And the glare in her eyes indicated she wasn't about to forgive and forget.

She sniffed again and wiped her nose on the back of her hand. I found a clean tissue in my coat pocket and handed it to her. She wiped her nose and eyes. "I had my passport already and some money saved, so I bought a ticket and made sure I was on the next plane after his took off."

"But how did you know where he would go? Did you see an itinerary or something like that?"

"No, but he didn't clear his computer search history. I could tell Nether Woodsmoor was the place he was most interested in, so I knew that was probably where he'd end up. But to make sure I didn't lose him, I put a tracking app on his phone."

"How did you do that?"

"I'm a paralegal, and we have a P.I. on retainer at the office. I told him I thought my boyfriend was sneaking around on me and that I wanted to track him. Kerry told me how to do it. It was easy. It only took a few seconds and then I knew exactly where Nick was all the time. As soon as I landed, I rented a car and followed him."

"Where did he go?"

She rolled her eyes. "A bunch of broken down old mansions."

"Do you remember the names of them?" I asked.

She released her hold on her knees, straightened her legs, and drew her phone out of her pocket. "Let's see, I have it all here in the logs of the tracking app. The day he arrived, he went to a hotel and stayed there. Slept off the time change, I guess. Then Thursday, the next day, he went to Sheffield. From there he went on to Ridgeford Court and Aslet House," she read.

I leaned a shoulder against the cold stone, mentally comparing the two estates with Parkview Hall. I'd researched those houses while working for the Jane Austen documentary, but Parkview was grander and better maintained than both of them. In fact, Ridgeford Court was a ruin. While Parkview Hall was classic Georgian, Ridgeford Court had been a medieval castle, and Aslet House was a Victorian's dream of towers, turrets, and decorative trim. "You're sure he wasn't into genealogy? Maybe he'd discovered some connection with his family and those historic places while he was going through his mom's things?"

"No, Nick was all about what was happening now. History was in the past and didn't matter. Well, except—" she rearranged her coat lapels, drawing them more closely around her neck. "I mean, no, he didn't care about history. He thought it was boring."

She reminded me of an actress I'd worked with on a location shoot after she got a phone call. She had been nearly vibrating with excitement, but she wouldn't talk about it. Several days later, she was announced as one of the leads in a popular movie sequel. Fern had that same barely contained air of secret knowledge.

She consulted her phone again. "He visited a few places in Sheffield before he went to the houses." Her eyebrows scrunched together. "He went to a place called The Butterfly House, which is essentially a zoo, and then to an enclosed garden." She shook her head. "I have no idea why he went to those places. He never wanted to go to the zoo or gardens before."

I had heard about the Sheffield's Winter Garden, an arcade of arches and glass, but had never been there. It was a modern take on the Victorian glass house. "Nick wasn't into architecture?" I asked, probing to see if Nick had tried the same lies with her that he had with my mom. "He told my mom he was studying it."

That made her laugh. "Nick? At school? And architecture?" She used the tissue to dab at her eyes. "Wow, that's the first good laugh I've had in days. Nick had no interest in building design—or school, either." She sobered. "At least I wasn't the only person he lied to. In an odd way that makes me feel a little better." She ran her hand over a dip in the rock. "He tried to call me that night, but I didn't answer." She lifted her chin and dusted her fingers on her coat. "If he was calling to apologize, then I wasn't having any of it. I would already be out of this dinky place, except the police came and said I couldn't leave here. You can't even call it a town. It's not big enough for that."

"I heard that Nick was...um...into drugs?"

"No." She shook her head. "He was a self-centered jerk—I've realized that now—but he was never into stuff like that."

"Not even marijuana?"

"No. Like I said, he wasn't into that."

What she'd said about Nick didn't go with what Marie had seen in his room at the inn, but Fern seemed so sure of herself. If Nick was using drugs, it seemed she didn't know about it.

The shadow reached the top of the hill and swept over us. "Come on, we better go down before it starts to rain." I pushed away from the rock, and Fern scooted off the ledge. I crossed the ridge, going as quickly as I could on the narrow path. I looked back and saw that Fern was following at a much slower pace. "You'll get drenched," I called.

"I don't care," she shouted back.

CHAPTER 15

"She was quite the drama queen," Alex said over the noise of the wipers as they swished back and forth, sweeping away the torrent of rain that pounded down on the windshield.

"Fern?" I looked up from my phone.

"Who else?"

"Sorry. I got a text from Ella. She says the organist, Sylvia, will be at Parkview at one to discuss an upcoming wedding. We can see her then." I had called Ella on our way to Hedgely and asked if she could put me in touch with Sylvia.

Alex checked the time. "We should be able to make it."

"Getting back to Fern," I said, "you're right. She definitely tends toward the melodramatic. She could have easily made it back and been inside the pub before the rain started." I was inside the cozy room with its warm fire when the first drops of rain splashed down. Fern came in a few minutes later, her hair plastered to her head and dripping down her back. I had introduced her to Alex and offered to buy her something warm to drink, but she waved me off, saying she wanted to be alone.

I'd already relayed to Alex what Fern had told me. "If Fern is telling the truth—and I'm inclined to believe her—then she doesn't have a clue about why Nick came here."

As the rain tapered off from a deluge to a steady patter, Alex turned the windshield wipers down. "You said Fern mentioned that Nick talked about coming into money. The prospect of big money would be enough to justify a trip from Los Angeles to England."

"It would. But where was Nick going to get the money? Another source of blackmail other than my mom?"

"That's my first thought," Alex said. "I talked to the barman, who is also the pub's owner, while you were gone, and it sounds like Fern has an alibi for Nick's death. Everyone noticed her return on Saturday night—lots of noisy crying—then she spent the rest of the night in her room. Her rental car didn't leave the parking area, which is right beside the owner's bedroom window. He says he's a light sleeper and would have heard if the car left."

"So unless she crept out silently and had someone else pick her up, she's not the murderer." I shook my head at my disappointed tone. "Listen to me. I'm sad that she's out of the running."

"That does seem a bit twisted, but I'll cut you some slack since it's your parents that you're worried about."

My phone rang. "It's Dad," I said as Alex turned the car between Parkview's gates. While Alex told the guy in the ticket kiosk that we were expected, I asked Dad, "How's the book-browsing?"

"Excellent. The Dickens was in good condition, only slightly foxed. I bought it...along with a few other things."

"I expected nothing less. Once you're in a bookstore, you're as susceptible as Mom is in a shoe store."

"Really? I better rein myself in, then."

"The difference is that you resale your book purchases."

"Most of them, yes. I don't think I'll be able to part with the Dickens, though." He lowered his voice. "I still have my minder with me. Stood out like a flashing neon light in the area around the bookshop. He lingered outside, window-shopping on the street, but there were only four actual businesses in operation. I considered inviting him into the shop, but restrained myself. I could have pointed out the especially fine books. Were you able to find the girlfriend?"

"Yes, but she wasn't as helpful as we'd hoped." Alex had parked the car in the Parkview's visitor lot. The rain was now more of gentle patter. I pressed the phone to my ear as Alex and I trekked through the raindrops to the staff entrance at the end of the west wing. I again summarized what I'd learned from Fern, telling Dad everything from Fern's misguided assumptions about who Ava was to Nick's tour of country homes, the zoo, and garden. Then I said, "I've got to go, Dad. Call me when you get back to Nether Woodsmoor."

"It will be later this afternoon. I think I'll do some sightseeing before I return."

Alex and I entered the suite of rooms that contained the estate offices of Parkview. The door to Beatrice's private office was open, but the lights were off.

Carl, his salt-and-pepper head bent over his desk with its usual avalanche of paper, looked up. Noticing my glance at Beatrice's office, he said, "Beatrice is still out."

"That's okay. I'm here to see Ella," I said, then added, "Good to see you back at work."

"Looks like you had plenty of 'get well' wishes." Alex gestured to several flower arrangements and potted plants that lined the edge of his desk, enclosing the piles of papers and binders.

He said, "I had no idea so many people cared."

"I'm not surprised." I noted that most of the names on the cards were female.

"How's Cart Cottage? Everything all right?" Carl asked.

"Yes, it's perfect," I said. "Thanks for the new flowers, by the way. They're gorgeous." Each day, a cleaner arrived at the cottage to tidy up. The flower arrangement in the kitchen had been changed out as well. Today we had an arrangement of peach roses, pink foxgloves, and peonies.

"You're welcome. We usually have a few kinks to work out with the first booking. I'm glad it's comfortable for you. Let me know if you need anything."

"We will," Alex said as we moved to Ella's desk at the back of the room. Malcolm's desk was empty, and I was glad that the back half of the room wasn't filled with people. Sylvia was seated in the chair beside Ella's desk. She wore a black turtleneck, jeans, and calf-high boots. Her golden brown hair fell in loose waves across her shoulders. Ella said hello to us, then said, "And you remember Sylvia?"

"Yes," I said. "In fact, we hoped we could ask you a few questions."

"Um—sure."

"How about some tea?" Ella asked. Before anyone could reply, she said, "I'll make a pot. Won't take a moment." She dragged another chair over for Alex, then waved me into her swivel chair before she moved to the alcove with the sink, small refrigerator, and hotplate.

I sat down in Ella's chair and looked at Alex, mentally telegraphing that I'd done all the talking last time. It was his turn.

"Again, I'm sorry about being late for the ceremony," Sylvia said.

"We're not worried about that," Alex said. "We wanted to talk to you about Nick."

The expression on her pretty face changed immediately. Some of the vivacity went out of it. "It's dreadful. I can't quite believe it, actually. We'd talked only a few hours before...it happened."

"You knew him well?" Alex asked, his voice gentle, but she stiffened.

"A little," she said.

Her guard was up. I recognized the signs—the sudden wariness in her gaze and the way she looked around for Ella.

Alex swiveled his chair toward me, and I knew he wanted me to join in the conversation. My family was involved. I had the most compelling argument to ask for her help, so I said, "I know it sounds strange for us to ask about him, but the police are investigating everyone who was here at Parkview late that night, which includes my parents. Alex and I are supposed to leave on our honeymoon soon, but if things are still up in the air about Nick...well, I don't think we'll be able to go. We're trying to find out anything we can that could wrap up the case. If you could tell us about Nick, that could be helpful. You knew him, right? He was a friend?"

"It was a long time ago. I don't know anything about him now," she said.

"You...dated?" I hazarded a guess.

She frowned. "How did you know that?"

I showed her the picture on my phone of the two of them. "It's one of the wedding photos. It's obvious that you hadn't just met."

She took my phone and stared at it a moment.

Alex said, "If you know anything about his past, that could help."

She returned the phone to me. "I met him about three years ago. I went out to California, sure I could 'make it.' Movies were my dream. I wanted to be the next Meryl Streep." She laughed. "Cliché, I know, but it's what I thought."

With her looks, I supposed if she'd gotten a break, she would have gone far.

"I met Nick at a party one night," she said. "We dated for a while. Maybe six weeks, then I ran out of money and decided it wasn't going to happen for me—at least not in Hollywood. I came home and got a job." She tapped the sheet music in her lap. "I still audition for parts, but teaching music and playing at weddings is how I pay the bills. That's all I can tell you. Nick and I had a good time, but it was over when I came back here. We didn't attempt a long-distance relationship. We had both moved on, I think."

She straightened the sheet music. "Anyway, I hadn't heard from him or been in touch with him at all since then. I was so surprised to see him at my table at the reception. He was as astonished as I was."

"What did you talk about?" Alex asked.

"We caught up." Her arched brows drew together in another frown. "But now that I think about it, he asked me loads of questions about my life, but whenever I asked him about what he was doing now, he was vague. He said he still lived in California and that he was in England checking out an investment opportunity."

I wanted to roll my eyes, but I managed to keep a straight face. Did Nick *ever* tell anyone the truth?

Alex asked, "What did he say about that business opportunity? Did he mention what it was? Or where he went to check it out?"

"No…" She was still frowning. "But there was something about the way he said it…almost like it was an inside joke."

"Did you see if he talked to anyone else at the reception? Did he seek anyone out?" Alex asked.

"Not really. We talked a little with some of the other people at the table, but not much. We spent most of the time catching up. He excused himself once and was gone for quite a while. I thought he'd probably gone to talk to someone else he knew. When he finally came back, I saw Malcolm hurry across the room to him. They spoke, but I didn't hear what they said."

"Did they argue?" I asked.

"No. It was a short exchange. Just a few sentences, I guess. Then Nick came back to the table, and we went on talking about what we were doing now—where we lived, that sort of thing. At the end of the evening, we talked about getting together again. We even exchanged phone numbers in the car park after he walked me to my car. It's all so sad to think what happened later."

"So he left at the same time you did?" I asked.

"Yes. He said he was going back to the village. When I think about driving away with him standing there...it gives me the shivers to think what happened later that night." She cleared her throat then shoved the sheet music in a leather carrying case. "I'm sorry I can't be more helpful." She zipped the case shut with a motion of finality as Ella returned with our tea. Sylvia stood. "I can't stay, Ella, I have another appointment." She turned to me. "I hope everything works out for you." She moved through the desks to the door, giving Carl a wave on her way out.

I gathered up a stack of papers from Ella's desktop so she could set down the tray with the tea, flipping closed the file folder that was on top. It had a neon pink sticker and the words "Flower Arrangement Examples" written on it. Even though I preferred coffee to tea, I had a cup of tea with Ella before we left.

When we left the estate office, I said to Alex, "I'd better check on my mom. See how she's doing—her migraine, you know."

"Sure. You seemed preoccupied back there," Alex said.

"I was, at the end." I described the folder that had been on top of Ella's desk. "I saw her frowning over the same folder before the wedding. I asked her about it then, and she glanced at Malcolm. It made me wonder..." My pace slowed as we moved down the long hallway toward the main block of the house.

"What?"

"The way Ella looked at him—it was odd. She looked...almost afraid, but then the moment was over, and I forgot about it until now. That folder didn't have examples of flower arrangements in it. It was open on her desk. I noticed it while we were talking to Sylvia. It was a spreadsheet, like the one Malcolm gave us with a breakdown of the wedding expenses. Ella handles publicity. Why would she be looking over a wedding expense spreadsheet?"

"Maybe they're shorthanded, and she's helping Malcolm."

"That could be, but it doesn't explain why she looked scared or why she locked it away in a drawer the first time I saw it."

CHAPTER 16

"*E*xcuse me," a voice said, and Alex and I both jumped. We were crossing the black-and-white marble floor of the entry hall to the staircase. I'd been so lost in my thoughts that I hadn't realized anyone else was near us. I looked around. I didn't see anyone, but then footsteps sounded, and a figure in a sweater vest emerged from the dim recess under the stairs. "Mr. and Mrs. Norcutt," Malcolm said, "I have three last-minute wedding gifts that have arrived here at Parkview since the wedding. Where should we deliver them?"

"You can send them to Ivy Cottage," Alex said while I wondered if Malcolm had overheard us. The high ceiling of the entry hall had a way of taking sounds, tossing them around, and creating interesting echoes.

"Very good," Malcolm said.

"Or we can take them with us now," I said.

"That's not necessary. We will see to the gift delivery."

I resisted the urge to ask if it was included in the Parkview event contract and said instead, "Oh, by the way, what did you and Nick talk about at the wedding reception?"

"Nick?" he asked.

"Someone said that you spoke to Nick Davis." I looked more closely at him. Was he blushing? I wished we were in a brighter area of the entry hall where I could see him better. He normally had a pasty complexion, and I'd never seen him with rosy cheeks.

"Oh, yes. The young man...who... the unfortunate young man." Malcolm drew in a deep breath. "He was upset with the parking arrangements. His car was blocked in. I told him he'd have to take it up with the groundskeepers when the event was over."

"So he wanted to leave early?" Alex asked.

Malcolm swallowed, took another deep breath, then said in a tone that indicated he had no interest in either Alex's questions or what Nick had done, "I have no idea. Excuse me." He walked across the hall, his posture upright and correct every step of the way.

"Yep, he certainly missed his calling. He's the embodiment of a snooty butler," I whispered as we climbed the steps to visit my mom in her room.

Alex and I were about halfway up the stairs when we heard a crash from below. We glanced at each other. Several banging sounds filled the air along with a groan. We turned and trotted back down the stairs and across the entry hall. The noise had come from the west wing. As soon as we entered the long corridor, we saw someone lying on the ground. A massive tapestry that had hung on the wall was now on the ground, partially covering the person.

Alex lifted the metal rod that the heavy tapestry hung from, pulling the woven fabric up and revealing Malcolm writhing on the floor, moaning. Alex angled the rod and heavy cloth out of the way. The metal pole clattered against the floor, an echo of the sound that we'd heard from the stairs.

I knelt beside Malcolm. His hands were over his abdomen, and between groans, he muttered, "Shiny...blue...why so many —" And then he clutched his midsection more tightly and gasped.

Alex and I exchanged an incredulous look. Formal, stuffy Malcolm muttering gibberish while writhing on the floor? Unthinkable. I knew he wouldn't want anyone to see him like this. I reached out a hand. "Malcolm?" He gripped it tightly, but couldn't seem to form any more words.

"We'll get help," I said and looked up at Alex.

He had his phone out and was dialing, but said, "The estate office might be faster, if Ella's still there. Are you okay to stay here with him?"

"Yes, go." I waved him on with my free hand, and Alex sprinted down the corridor.

Malcolm groaned again then managed to utter a few words. I leaned closer. Had he said something about a man and hawks?

"Can I do anything, Malcolm? What can I do to help?"

He didn't respond, and I wondered if I should loosen his tie. His face and hands were clammy, and beads of sweat had popped out along his high forehead. Fortunately, at that moment, Ella and Alex came running back. I could hear more pounding foot-falls coming from the other direction, too. In seconds, my hand had been pried from Malcolm's grip, and two people in Parkview's navy blazers had taken over, checking Malcolm's vital signs and murmuring reassuring things to him.

Alex and I got out of the way. It wasn't long before an ambulance arrived, and Malcolm was strapped to a gurney. After a short consultation with Ella, the medical personnel decided it would be easiest to take Malcolm out Parkview's main doors because they were the closest. The tall double doors were thrown open, and he was wheeled out, then carefully transported down one of the curved staircases. Alex and I watched from the entry hall as the ambulance pulled away, bumping over the gravel of the circular sweep in front of the house.

"What is all the commotion about?" asked a voice at my shoulder.

"Mom, what are you doing up? I thought you had a migraine."

"I did." She touched her temple, brushing back the shock of white hair. "Last night was awful, but I'm feeling much better now. I had a delightful lunch with Malcolm. I invited him to eat with me when I saw he was also dining alone. He's not that bad once you get around that starchy personality."

"The ambulance was for him," I said.

Mom looked out the open front doors. The ambulance was still visible, its lights flashing against the tree trunks as it made its way down the drive. "No! What happened?"

"I don't know. It was some sort of attack." From the way Malcolm had clutched his stomach, I suspected food poisoning, but I didn't want to say anything about that to Mom and scare her, especially if they ate lunch together. Alex picked up on my warning glance and didn't go into any more details about Malcolm.

"No wonder he didn't eat much at lunch," Mom said. "It must have been coming on then."

"Did he seem ill?" Alex asked.

"He didn't touch the dessert, and I asked him if he was feeling all right. He said he had a bit of an upset stomach but told me not to worry about it. I do hope he's okay." Mom frowned. "He said he'd make sure I got a complimentary jar of the vinaigrette that was on the salad. Lemon and honey. Not too heavy. It's made here at Parkview. So many of these salad dressings are overpowering, but this one was perfect."

"I'm sure Ella or someone else can take care of it, if Malcolm can't," I said, thinking how absurd it was to be standing here chatting about salad dressing when Malcolm was in bad shape and being taken to the hospital.

The front doors were still open, and when the Range Rover drove up and parked at the foot of one of the staircases, it drew Mom's attention. "There's my ride," she said and started for the doors.

"You're going out?" The fact that Mom had her guidebook and umbrella with her finally registered.

"Just into the village to look around. Neal said he'd give me a little tour. I haven't seen much of Nether Woodsmoor, you know, with the shopping and getting ready for the wedding. I thought I'd look around today. It's too late to go anywhere else. Because I wasn't feeling well, I delayed my day trip to London until tomorrow. Should we get together for dinner tonight? Or would you two rather be alone? Just let me know." She fluttered her fingers as she left.

"And to think that I was worried about her filling her time while she was here," I said. "At least she's getting to use her umbrella." The fabric burst into a taut canopy that she held aloft to protect her from the light rain as she went down the stairs.

"She's quite the tourist," Alex said. "But she didn't even ask about the investigation," he added with a raised eyebrow.

"That's my mom all over. She throws herself wholeheartedly into whatever she does. If she's sightseeing, she goes the whole way—money belt, guidebook, and tours. I sort of admire that about her. But," I sighed, "when she's immersed in one thing, everything else doesn't exist."

Ella slipped inside the tall doors before a man in a navy blazer closed them. Her hands were clasped together and she looked worried as she crossed the entry hall to us. "Malcolm lost consciousness right before the ambulance left. That's not a good sign, is it?"

"I don't know," I said, but thought she was probably right.

"I heard them say that his pulse was high and that he was in shock. What happened? Do you know?"

"No, we found him collapsed in the west corridor," I said.

Alex added, "He'd spoken to us a moment before and seemed his usual self."

"Except he was a little flushed. And my mother said he had an upset stomach at lunch."

My phone rang. "It's Louise," I said, surprised to see her name. I'd been so busy with the wedding and the guests that I'd only had snatches of conversation with her during the last few weeks.

"Kate," she said when I answered. "I am so sorry to call you, but I don't know what else to do. Shannon has—well—she's fallen apart. I finally got her to stop crying, but she shaking and scared. She won't tell me what's wrong. She says she'll only talk to you—that you're the only one who can help. Normally, I'd call her parents and have them sort her out, but she has had a bit of a rough time. Her family is…not helpful, let's say. I hate to ask, but could you come talk to her? The only thing I can get out of her is that it's something to do with that man who was killed in the maze."

"I'll be right there."

*a*s Louise opened the door to her office, Shannon jumped and moved her hand away from her mouth.

Louise said to her, "Kate's here, luv. Tell her what's bothering you."

Shannon's fingernails were jagged, and her cuticles looked raw. She closed her fingers into a fist, hiding her bitten nails and looked at me with wide eyes. Louise closed the door behind us. I looked around for a place to sit. Since Shannon was huddled in the chair behind Louise's desk—the only seat—I perched on the edge of the desk. As Alex and I had walked into the pub a few minutes earlier, Alex's phone had rung with a call from Grace. He'd dropped back to take it, waving for me to go ahead without him.

"What's wrong, Shannon?" I hoped it wouldn't be too long before Alex poked his head into the room and checked on us. His soothing attitude would go a long way to calming Shannon. She blinked her swollen eyelids and sniffed. Beyond the obvious signs of tears, her attitude had changed too. She looked like she had when she first came to work for Louise, frightened and worried.

"No one will believe me." Her hand strayed back to her

mouth, but then she quickly crossed her arms over her abdomen in a defensive posture. "They won't believe me. They won't. I can't go to the police. They'll think that I was in on it somehow. They twist your words and try to prove things that aren't true—that's what Dad said."

I tried to sort out her rambling statements and failed. "I'm a bit confused. Why don't you start with what upset you. It happened today?"

She unclasped one skinny arm and nudged a newspaper on the desk. "I saw that."

It was the new issue of the local weekly paper, which was a thin stack of newsprint pages, folded in half, tabloid style. Usually the local "news" consisted of updates about events like garden shows or the schedule for the Guy Fawkes fireworks display. The announcement of an independent cheesemaker leasing a shop on the high street was considered hard news, but this issue, the first since Nick's death, carried a grainy image of Nick Davis along with the headline, *American Killed While on Holiday*. "And it upset you?" I asked, feeling my way.

She nodded. "I didn't know it was him until today. All I'd heard was that a man had been killed. I'd heard the name, but didn't realize..." She sniffled and squeezed her locked arms tighter around her waist.

"So you saw his picture, and it shocked you?" When Louise walked me back to the office, she'd said that Shannon dropped a tray of dishes and hadn't been coherent since then. In a small village like Nether Woodsmoor, it would be possible to not see a photo of the man who was killed. Everyone would know about the death of course, but if it rated a mention on the television news at all, it would only be in passing. The headlines of news broadcasts were focused on the bigger cities. And I doubted that Shannon, who was in her early twenties, got her news from the local nightly newscasts anyway. If the man's face had shown up on Facebook or some other social media outlet, then she might have seen it.

"Yes, I had no idea that it was Nicolas."

"Nicolas?"

"That's what he said his name was, not Nick, like it says in the article."

"So you knew him as Nicolas?"

She nodded a confirmation. "Yes, just Nicolas. I never knew his last name."

"How did you meet him? Was it in the pub last week?"

"No, it was during the summer."

I felt my eyebrows rise in surprise as I said, "Nick—I mean Nicolas—was here, in Nether Woodsmoor, during the summer?" If he was, that was an interesting new angle. We'd thought that this was Nick's first visit to Nether Woodsmoor. If he'd been here before, it opened up all sorts of questions. Did he know anyone in the village other than Shannon? Was he returning to visit someone this time?

"Yes."

"You're sure it was him?" I tapped the photo in the newspaper.

"I'm positive. His hair was a little shorter than it is in the picture, but it's him. It's Nicolas."

"Okay. How did you meet him?"

"It was when I was helping out at Parkview in August. I worked there for extra hours. It's their busy time, you know. Mornings, I worked here at the pub, then I went over to Parkview in the afternoon. I helped in the estate office, answering calls and filing papers."

I nodded. It wasn't surprising that Shannon had taken on extra work at Parkview during the summer. Most people in the village had some sort of tie to the stately home. Either they worked there themselves, or they had a relative or friend who worked there. It was the largest employer in the area.

"One day, I was leaving the estate office and this guy was

wandering around, lost. He'd gotten separated from his tour. I helped him find the group, but the tour was over. They were in the gift shop. He offered to buy me a cup of tea."

Nick and his cups of coffee and tea, I thought. He must have used the line a lot. And hadn't Ella said that Nick had told her he was lost on the night of the wedding? His pattern of behavior—lying and getting lost—didn't seem to vary. "What was he like?"

"He was nice." Shannon had relaxed a little. She'd uncrossed her arms and now sat less stiffly. "He said he was here doing research for a book."

"Of course he did."

"What?"

"Never mind. What else did he say?"

"His research was all about...um...what was it? The economics of the country home in modern times, I think. Something like that, anyway. He was interested in Parkview. How it was set up, what it was like to work there, that sort of thing."

I swung a foot as I balanced on the desk. "Can you remember what sorts of questions he asked? Anything specific?"

"Well, he wanted to know how long Parkview was open. How big the crowds are. When the busy time of the year was. How many people were on staff. What my job was like. Stuff like that."

"Couldn't he find some of that out online?" I asked.

"That's what I told him. I said he should set up an interview with someone like Mr. Stewart or maybe even Beatrice. They could tell him so much more than I could, but he said that he'd wait on that. Right then he wanted an insider look, the perspective of an average employee."

I made a murmuring sound of encouragement to keep her talking, but as a part-time temporary hire, Shannon was hardly a typical employee.

"He was interested in everything, really. He had lots of questions about the estate office, and how it worked, and everyone who worked there."

"So he asked detailed questions about the office?"

"Yes, he even wanted to know if we got breaks and what we did on them. If we could eat in the restaurant or bring in our own food, and if we ever had to work overtime. What our schedules were like, did anyone have to do shift work—that sort of thing."

"That seems sort of odd for a book on country homes."

"He said he wasn't sure what would go in the book and what would be left out, so he wanted as much information as he could get to start with. He said you never know what will be valuable."

I made another murmuring noise, wondering what Nick's game had been.

"He even got my email and phone number. For follow-up questions, he said, but I never heard from him again. And then when I saw his picture in the paper and realized he was the dead bloke in the maze—I panicked, I guess. I don't want anything to do with the police. Dad always says they make a mush of everything and try to confuse you and take what you say and twist it—"

"Shannon, calm down." I put a hand on her shoulder. She'd shifted back to nervous and edgy, her voice rising with each phrase. "It's going to be okay. I know Quimby. You can trust him. He'll want to hear what you told me—"

"But he might think I did it. Why else would I have kept quiet until now—*days* after Nicolas was killed? He'll think I was involved somehow, I know it."

Her voice was creeping up again so I said sharply, "Where were you on Saturday night? Late, like between ten and midnight?"

She frowned, and I could tell she was mentally running back through the days. "At home with my mum," she finally said.

"So she can vouch for you, that you were home all evening?"

"Yes. We started watching a show, and it rolled into the next episode when one finished. I think we watched about four. It was one in the morning before we finally turned it off."

"Then you're fine. You weren't anywhere near the maze when the murder happened. You can tell the police what happened and not worry. I promise it will be okay. DCI Quimby is a good guy. He's smart and thorough and will treat you right."

"Okay...but only if you stay with me. Will you do that?"

"Yes, I'll stay if DCI Quimby will let me, but he might want to talk to you by yourself."

She breathed a little easier. "I'll insist."

I sent Quimby a text with the news that Shannon had met Nick earlier this summer.

He texted back. *Yes, we know he was in the area at that time. Keep her there. I'll be there shortly.*

With their ability to gather information, I should have realized that the police would already know about Nick's earlier visit to Nether Woodsmoor. They had probably already checked his flights, his credit cards, and his phone records.

Quimby arrived about fifteen minutes later, his face serious and manner solemn. Shannon was still seated behind Louise's desk, but she looked more composed than she had earlier. Louise had insisted she have a cup of tea and a scone. For any sort of problem, food and a cup of tea were always part of the solution according to Louise.

I introduced Quimby to Shannon, glad that she looked more like her usual self. Quimby nodded his thanks to me and indicated I should leave.

"Can't Kate stay?" Shannon asked.

"I'm afraid not," Quimby said in a tone that left no room for pleading. "There's nothing to worry about," he said to Shannon, his tone softening. "I only want to hear about what you know about Nick Davis. Anything you can tell us will be a help." Louise had added an extra cup to the tea tray, and Quimby poured himself a cup then held the teapot out to Shannon. "More tea?"

"Ah—sure."

"It won't take more than a few minutes, and then you'll be on your way," Quimby said as he poured. He reached for his cup, then settled down across the desk from Shannon, using a stack of boxes as a makeshift chair. "We'll chat for a few minutes. What you have to tell us could be extremely valuable." His tone indicated it was a conversation, not an interrogation. Shannon looked reassured, and I closed the door.

I returned to the pub and spotted Alex. "How's Grace? I hope they have better weather than this." I slid into the chair beside him and glanced outside. The gray clouds still lingered, but the rain had tapered off to a drizzle, spotting the windows.

"It's clear where they are, but I think she'd have a great time even in a downpour. She's riding every roller coaster she can find, and she's seen all the shows—*all* the shows, Dad emphasized. He said he hasn't had such a rigorous schedule since the prime minister came to visit Chile. I ordered lunch for us. Sandwich sound good?"

"Delicious."

Ella came into the pub and hurried across to us. Droplets of water dotted her hair, and the shoulders of her long-sleeved pink oxford were saturated. "What's wrong?" I asked as Alex pulled out a chair for her, but she didn't sit down.

"Where is DCI Quimby? They said he was here?"

"He's in Louise's office, but he'll be out soon. What's wrong, Ella? Why don't you sit down?" She looked like she might fall down, if she didn't sit soon. I'd never noticed that she had freckles, but a few stood out bright against her washed-out skin. She held a folder in the crook of her arm, her knuckles white where she gripped the edge of it.

She looked at the back of the pub. "I really should talk to him right away."

"I promise you, he doesn't want to be interrupted. He's interviewing someone."

"Oh. Okay." She perched on the edge of the chair. She kept the folder clasped tightly to her chest and looked like she was ready to leap up the moment Quimby appeared. Louise stopped at the table. "Ella, you look shell-shocked. Can I bring you something?"

Ella glanced around as if she'd forgotten she was inside the pub, but she knew Louise well enough not to turn down her offer. "Tea, I suppose." Her tone indicated that the kind of beverage didn't matter at all.

Louise gave her a concerned look, then shifted her glance to Alex and me, clearly indicating we should sort out what was bothering Ella.

"What's wrong, Ella?" I asked again, and this time instead of ignoring me, she blinked quickly. "Malcolm was poisoned."

CHAPTER 18

"*P*oisoned?" I asked. "How do you know? Are you sure?"

She nodded, her fingers flexing tighter around the folder. "The hospital called. Malcolm doesn't have anyone—no relatives, so they called Parkview to ask some questions and give us a report. Of course, with Beatrice still gone, I said I'd take it since I work with him all the time. The hospital said they're still sorting out what exactly it was." Her fingers trembled as she used her free hand to brush her hair behind her ear. "I feel terrible now." She lowered her voice. "You know what he's like. So difficult. There were days that I actually thought it would be nice if he'd just go away. But to think of him now in the hospital, all alone… It must be awful for him. Who would do something like that?"

Alex and I exchanged a silent glance. It had to be related to Nick's death. I'm sure my face looked as troubled as Alex's. He twisted around and called to Louise, "Ella needs something stronger with that tea. She's had a shock."

"Let's not jump to conclusions," I said to Ella.

"Right," Alex said. "Are they sure it wasn't food poisoning?"

"No, something about his reaction. They said it was more likely he was poisoned."

She looked so distressed. "Then maybe it was just a mistake," I said in an effort to soothe her. "Did Malcolm take any medicine? Maybe he mixed up some tablets or something."

Ella shook her head so adamantly that her hair whipped around. "No. That's something they asked about before they took him away in the ambulance. I've never seen him take any prescriptions. He makes a point of living clean, and he makes sure everyone knows about it. You saw his smoothies. Everything has to be organic, pure, no additives, no preservatives. I thought he was off his head, but he always makes a big deal about all-natural ingredients being better. He won't even take an aspirin. He says a glass of water—filtered, of course—can cure most headaches."

"I'm glad this subject didn't come up when my mother was around him," I said. She would have had a thing or two to tell him about migraines.

Louise arrived with tea as well as a glass with a little brandy, which she commanded Ella to drink first. She did and made a face after she swallowed. "Hand me that tea," she said hoarsely between coughs. "I definitely need it now." She swallowed a few sips, and her shoulders relaxed an inch.

When she recovered her equilibrium, Ella said, "They know it was some sort of poison. Something to do with his symptoms."

Alex took out his phone and began to type as Ella added, "I don't know how they'll ever trace it, if it was in his food at lunch. The dishes are washed and put away. Any leftover food has been disposed of in the garbage. It's all in one big…well, pile." She took a longer sip of her tea. "I'm so thankful no one else got sick."

I wasn't listening to Ella at that point. I was stuck on the thought of who Malcolm's lunch companion had been. I reached for my phone and dialed Mom's number. I listened to it ring with a sinking feeling, telling myself that she didn't like to answer her phone and that she usually ignored it or had it turned off. I was about to hang up when the ringing stopped, and a voice said, "Kate, why are you calling me? I'm in the middle of paying for the cutest pair of shoes."

I leaned back in my chair and tilted the phone to speak to Alex, who had looked up from his phone to watch me. "She's exactly the same as she always is." I shifted back to speaking into the phone. "I'm just checking on you. How are you feeling?"

"Fine. I told you the migraine is gone."

"I remember, but nothing else is bothering you?"

Alex consulted his phone and said in a low voice, "I think I found it. Digitalis—signs of overdose...irregular pulse, vision changes, loss of consciousness."

"Any heart flutters or trouble seeing?"

"Kate, hold on," Mom said, her voice impatient.

I tilted the phone away from my mouth and said to Alex, "What does it say about vision changes?"

"It doesn't give any details."

"Well, maybe that explains what Malcolm was saying. Maybe he saw flashes or something. I thought he was confused, but he said the word shiny and then later something about a man with a hawk."

Ella tilted her head. "It couldn't have been Guy Fawkes, that he said, could it?"

"Oh—the fireworks. Yes...it could have. His words weren't clear, but...yes, I think that might have been what he said. Maybe he was seeing flashes of lights and it made him think of the fireworks display."

Mom's voice came back on the line "Okay, Kate. What did you ask?"

I repeated my questions.

"No. Why do you ask? I'm feeling fine. Well, a tad worried about how I'll get these shoes in my suitcase, but I can always mail them—"

"Dizziness?" I persisted.

"No, Kate. It's so rude to interrupt people, you know."

"Are you seeing flashes of light or brightness?"

"On a dreary day like today? Of course not."

I whispered to Alex, "Does it say how long before symptoms start?"

"Immediately, it looks like."

"Kate," Mom said in my ear. "What is this about?"

"It's bad news about Malcolm Stewart. He was..." I hesitated then decided there wasn't an innocuous way to say it. "He was poisoned. Since you had lunch with him, I wanted to make sure you were okay."

"That is awful. And to think I was chatting with him only a little while ago. Was it in something he ate?"

"It appears that way," I said.

"Then I'm so glad I didn't have the fish."

"You had a different meal?" I asked.

"Soup and salad. It was exactly what I needed. Something light after not feeling well."

"You didn't share anything? Not even a bite?"

"No, definitely not. Oh, there's Neal. He parked up the street, and he doesn't see me. I'll call you after I get back to Parkview." The dial tone sounded in my ear.

"No need to worry about her," I said, but couldn't completely squash the concern I felt.

Alex looked at me with concern. "You doing okay?"

"Not really. That could be Mom in the hospital, and she doesn't even realize it." My stomach flip-flopped. "What if it *was* meant for Mom? The police already think she's involved in Nick's murder. She would make a convenient scapegoat if..."

I didn't realize I'd reached for Alex's hand until he squeezed mine. "But that's not what happened," he said. "She had a different meal, right?"

"Malcolm had the fish. Mom had soup and salad."

"Then it's not like they were served the same meal and the waitress mixed up the plates."

"I know, but I can't help but think about it." My mind spiraled through different scenarios. "This, on top of the feather—" I stopped speaking, not sure if I should go on with Ella listening. Did anyone else know about the blue feather other than the investigators and my family?

"It changes everything," Alex agreed, and his eyes told me he understood my train of thought. "Let me see if we can delay our departure. I can call Dad's assistant and check on the flexibility of our travel dates."

"I don't know—it's our honeymoon..."

"Venice will still be there in a few weeks, and if we go now, neither one of us would enjoy it."

"If they even let us go." I nodded reluctantly. "Postponing is probably the best call."

"I have to get the number for Dad's assistant from the cottage. It's in the paperwork in my suitcase."

"I better stay here and see how things go with Shannon and Quimby."

"Then I'll run out to the cottage and come back." He stood. As he kissed my cheek, he whispered, "We'll get it all sorted, *then* we'll go to Venice."

After he left, Ella said, "He is such a great guy."

I watched him go, his tall figure almost filling the doorway as he left. "No question about that. He is." I smiled briefly then noticed that Ella had placed the folder she'd been clutching to her chest on the table. I recognized the sticker on the outside. "You were working on that file when you looked so worried before the wedding." She wouldn't come through the rain without a jacket and clutching the file to talk to Quimby unless... "Do you think it has something to do with Malcolm?"

"I don't know." Her tone was miserable.

CHAPTER 19

"*I*'ve been trying to figure it out for weeks." She took another sip of her tea and drew a long breath. "Let me tell you about it. It will help me organize my thoughts so that when I talk to DCI Quimby, I won't sound like an incoherent busybody. I don't want to waste his time. I'm not sure if it's anything at all."

"What did you find?" I asked.

"It wasn't me. It was Shannon. She worked in the office at Parkview this summer—a temporary hire."

"She told me about it."

"Shannon did a great job. She answered phones for us and did odd jobs, all those things that get pushed down the list—filing and sorting and clearing out. She was working on some files for Malcolm one day. She finished the stack that he'd given her. She went back to his desk and picked up the next pile of papers. Malcolm had been called away for a few minutes. When he returned and saw what she was working on, he lost it. He's always fussy and particular, but this time…" Her fingers worried up and down the crease of the folder. "I've never seen him like that. His face—he was so angry. He shouted at her. He has a lot of faults, but he's never raised his voice. At least, I'd never seen him behave that way until then."

Ella tapped one of the pages that had slid out back into the folder. "You know what Shannon's like. She's a timid little thing. Malcolm frightened her so badly that she dropped the papers. They scattered all over the floor, and I hopped up to help her pick them up. Malcolm couldn't get the papers out of my hands fast enough, which was weird because they were only purchase forms and invoices for events. Nothing top secret. But I noticed he put them away immediately. After that incident, he always put them in his lower desk drawer and kept it locked."

She took a gulp of her tea, then rushed through her next words, a guilty expression on her face. "One night I stayed late and copied them."

"How did you get to them?" I had a hard time picturing Ella picking a lock.

"Malcolm's desk is the same model as Carl's. He never locks his desk, but he keeps his keys in the middle desk drawer. I waited until they were both gone, then tried Carl's desk keys on Malcolm's desk. They worked on every drawer. I took the papers, copied them, then put everything back exactly as it was." She put a hand over her forehead, shading her eyes, then peeked out from behind her hand. "I know it was wrong to take them, but I didn't feel like I could go to Beatrice without concrete proof that something was wrong. His reaction—" She pressed her palm against her forehead for a second then leaned forward and braced her elbows on the table. "I can't explain it, but I thought something was...off. I knew we'd had a complaint or two about some charges..."

She sighed. "He's my direct superior. I report to him, so I didn't want it to look like I was...um...trying to get rid of him."

"Beatrice wouldn't think that about you."

She tilted her head one way then the other. "Maybe. You know what happened when I was hired, right?"

"Um...no. All I know is that you were hired. Is there more?"

Ella leaned back in her chair then traced her finger along the rim of her teacup. "I interviewed with Beatrice for the job at Parkview. She wanted to hire me, and I thought I'd gotten the publicity job. But then Beatrice decided that the job was too much for one person and created two positions. She brought on Malcolm and gave him the director of publicity position."

"With you as the assistant," I said.

"I was disappointed at the time, but even I could see that Malcolm was more experienced than me. I understand why Beatrice gave him the top job. But with that background...Beatrice knew I was disappointed with the way it worked out. I didn't want her—or Malcolm—to think I was trying to undermine him. And if there *was* something...off... about the forms, if Malcolm was fiddling with the numbers, then you know Beatrice."

"She's not one to wait around," I said. "She'd go immediately to Malcolm."

"Exactly. My fear was that if he *was* doing something shady, then he might have different records he could produce that would look perfectly innocent. I could lose my job." Ella leaned back in her chair. "It's such a relief to talk about this. I've been sorting through these papers trying to figure out what to do for weeks."

"So *is* he fiddling with the numbers?"

"I think so. I've found a couple of duplicate invoices, places where it's obvious even to me that he's skimmed some money. He showed an expense for flowers at one wedding that was several hundred more than the amount on the actual invoice from the florist."

"That's not good." Parkview often handled all the vendors for events. A bride and groom could pay one fee to Parkview and concentrate on their wedding. They didn't have to worry about juggling multiple vendors for the big day. If you used the vendors from their approved list, Parkview—that is, Malcolm—handled it all and sent you the final bill. If you wanted to pick your own vendors, you could do that, too. But I bet most people went with the more hassle-free approach of using the recommended vendors.

"And Beatrice would be so upset if Malcolm was doing that." Ella lowered her voice. "If word got out, it could ruin our reputation as a luxury wedding venue." She returned to her normal tones, but still spoke quietly enough that she wouldn't be overheard. "What I don't know is if what I found was intentional, or was it a few innocent mistakes? I only have a few weeks' worth of papers. I've been trying to search the older files, but it's hard to find a time when Malcolm isn't in."

"Did you talk to Lucas about it?" I wondered what her constable boyfriend thought of the situation.

"No, I didn't tell anyone. I wanted to be sure before I said anything, but now...well, I have to tell the police."

"Yes, I think you do," I said, my mind was already spinning through what Ella's revelations and the poisoning could mean.

~

"But does Malcolm's possible creative accounting have anything to do with Nick's death?" I said to Alex as I finished recounting what Shannon and Ella had told me at the pub.

Alex turned the MG's windshield wipers off. "That is the big question."

As soon as Shannon emerged from Louise's office, Ella had darted back there to catch Quimby. Shannon had tied on her apron and circulated through the tables. Business had been picking up at the pub as it got later in the day and despite Louise saying that Shannon should go home, she'd insisted on finishing her shift. Ella was still closeted in the office when Alex returned to the pub to pick me up.

"You think Nick threatened to expose Malcolm's skimming, and Malcolm killed Nick?" Alex asked.

"It wouldn't be the first time Nick blackmailed someone."

"No," Alex said as we cruised through the gates at Parkview. I wanted to see Mom face-to-face and try to impress on her the possible danger that she might be in. The man in the kiosk had seen us so often that he waved us on without even stopping us.

"You know we've been here too much, when they don't even attempt to charge you an entrance fee," I said, momentarily distracted, but my thoughts went right back to Malcolm. "But how could Nick know about the skimming? Ella isn't even sure it's actually going on."

"Sometimes the appearance of impropriety is all it takes," Alex said. "Did Ella tell anyone?"

"No one at all."

"What about Shannon? She might have noticed the invoices when she dropped them. Nick wanted to stay in touch with Shannon. Suppose he contacted her later, and she told him about it?"

"I could be wrong, but I don't think Shannon suspected anything was off with the invoices. I think if she had, she would have mentioned it when she told me about meeting Nick. And she said he hadn't gotten in touch later."

"Then it sounds like it doesn't have any connection to Nick."

The fine mist of rain continued to coat everything with additional layers of dampness, and the gray sky still loomed overhead. In the thick shade of the trees that lined the drive it almost felt like late evening.

"I looked up more about digitalis while I was waiting on Dad's admin," Alex said. "It's used for—"

I shifted toward him and grabbed his arm. "I completely forgot you went to check on changing the travel dates. I'm a terrible wife. I'm so wrapped up in this stuff around Nick and now Malcolm that everything else sort of goes out of focus for me. And that's awful—especially since I'm on my honeymoon. I'm so sorry, Alex—sorry about all of it. That this has happened, and that we're caught up in it, and that it's taken over our honeymoon."

Alex stopped the car under the arch of tree branches and then turned to me. "It's not your fault that Nick got killed. From what we've learned about him, I think he brought that on himself."

"But that doesn't change the fact that this has got to be the worst honeymoon ever," I said. "Chasing around after people we barely know to ask them what they can tell us about a man we never met."

"It's not exactly how I pictured our honeymoon, I'll give you that, but the good news is that we do have some flexibility on our travel dates. I said to cancel our flight and reservations for Tuesday and that I'd call back when we were ready to rebook everything. Dad got travel insurance, or his assistant did."

"Thank goodness for that," I said.

"I don't think it's the *worst* honeymoon ever." Alex tucked a strand of my hair behind my ear and caressed my cheek with his thumb. "If we were shouting and screaming and couldn't get along that would be far worse. We're together. That's the important thing. We'll get through this. And I like your concentrated focus." He smiled at me slowly. "Once this is wrapped up—and it will be, we'll see to that—then I want you to focus all your energy on us."

I leaned into his hand and closed my eyes, enjoying the feel of his palm against my cheek. "I like that plan." I realized I sounded a bit breathless. I opened my eyes and found him studying me with that intense gaze of his that made the rest of the world fade away.

"Glad we agree on that," Alex said as he leaned in to kiss me.

A while later we both became aware of an annoying beeping sound and broke apart. Headlights lit up the interior of our car. Alex glanced in the rearview mirror at the grill of an oversized

SUV that was so close it looked as if it had parked on top of the MG's bumper. "I guess we'd better move."

Another long blast on the car horn sounded. "That's a shame." I threw him a flirty smile. "We were just getting to the good part."

"Don't worry. We'll get back there later." Alex waved an apology to the car behind us, then put the MG in gear. "So…let's see. Where were we? There was something I was going to tell you before we were distracted in such a pleasant way."

"After that kiss, I'm having trouble remembering why we came to Parkview in the first place."

Alex sent me a wicked grin. "To check on your mom."

"That's right…Oh, you were about to tell me something about what poisoned Malcolm."

He nodded and turned serious. "I found out it's used for people with heart problems. Sounds like it's fairly common. It strengthens the heartbeat, which can actually help people with heart issues. Too much of it, and then you get the symptoms that Malcolm had."

"Digitalis, you said." I checked my lipstick in the side mirror then reached for my purse.

"That's right," Alex said, sounding surprised that I remembered.

"It's a poison that shows up in a lot of mysteries," I explained. "I think Agatha Christie used it several times in her novels."

"And my sister reads them. Now there is a truly frightening thought."

I capped my lipstick and punched his arm playfully. "Grace likes the intellectual challenge of solving the puzzle in mysteries."

"Grace always wants to be the smartest person in the room."

"Everyone likes to feel like that." I put my lipstick away and sighed. "I certainly don't feel smart right now. Befuddled is more like it. Everyone we've been concentrating on as possible suspects seems a bit young to have a heart problem."

"That's true. Fern and Sylvia are certainly probably around

what? Twenty-five?" I nodded my agreement, and Alex went on, "And, while I don't think Shannon or Ella is involved, they're young, too."

"I suppose someone—any of them could have a weak heart. It doesn't have to be an older person. I mean, Carl just had a scare about his heart, and I don't think of him as old—" Alex and I looked at each other. "Do you think...?"

"That Carl's involved?" Alex asked. "I suppose it depends on what sort of medicine he's on for his heart problem."

Could it be possible? Could Carl have knifed Nick and poisoned Malcolm? "I suppose he could have done it," I said, working it out as I spoke. "Carl was at the wedding, and he works with Malcolm...but why? Why would he kill Nick? Did Carl ever meet Nick?"

"Who knows? I guess there is a chance that Carl did it," Alex said, but his tone was doubtful. "It doesn't feel right."

"I agree." I leaned forward and squinted as we emerged from the trees and Parkview's facade came into view. "Is that—? Yes, it's got to be my mom. No one else has a black umbrella that large."

"And it doesn't look good," Alex said. Constable Albertson was escorting my mom down the stairs to a waiting police car.

CHAPTER 20

*A*lex didn't bother to drive to the parking area where we normally left the car. He pulled to a stop behind the police car.

I jumped out as Constable Albertson and my mom had reached the bottom of the steps. He released her arm.

"What is going on?" I crunched across the gravel, blinking the mist out of my eyes.

"Don't look so worried, dear," Mom said from under the black canopy of her umbrella. "They have a few more questions for me, that's all."

Albertson opened the back door of the police car. "I'm taking her to the incident room at the church hall."

"We'll meet you there," I said to her.

She tucked the damp umbrella next to her feet. "I'm sure there's no need to do that."

"Yes, there is." I was already walking back to the car where Alex stood beside the open driver's door.

We got caught at a light, and by the time we arrived at the church hall, I didn't see Constable Albertson or my mom anywhere. The high-ceilinged room echoed with the voices of the investigators as they worked at desks made from long tables that were usually covered with white cloths and displayed platters of cookies for village events. The church hall had been used as an incident room once before, and I had the same feeling that I'd stepped onto a location shoot. Like a film set, it had the air of a temporary workspace as well as the general low-level buzz of hectic activity. I spotted Albertson returning alone from the back of the hall. He moved through the maze of desks, tables, and folding chairs, stepping across power cords that crisscrossed the floor. The church hall was a newer building than the nearby church—by several hundred years—but the hall was built in a time when typewriters hadn't been invented.

The wooden floors squeaked with Albertson's heavy tread. "Your mum is with Quimby in the offices in the back. He said no one else is allowed in," he added.

"Oh." I shot a worried glance at Alex. Who knew what Mom would say?

"It's about Malcolm, isn't it?" I asked. Albertson knew Alex and me, and I hoped our past interactions gave us a little credit with him. He might feel comfortable talking about the investigation with us. "Can you tell us anything about what's going on?"

"We're not treating it as accidental."

"Oh," I said, again, feeling as if half the air had been sucked out of my lungs. That was not a good answer for my mom. Alex reached for my hand, and I was glad to feel the warmth of his fingers. He asked, "How is Malcolm? Do you know?"

"Expected to recover. He may be able to leave the hospital tomorrow."

"Was Malcolm able to tell you anything else?" I asked. "After he had lunch with my mom, did he do anything else? See anyone else? Have a cup of tea, maybe?"

"I'm afraid not," Albertson said. "He said he met you in the entry hall immediately after he left the conservatory." Food was usually served either on the terrace with the view of the gardens or indoors in the conservatory. On soggy days like today, the food service moved completely inside in the conservatory.

My face must have shown my worry because Albertson said, "Your mum isn't the only person who was near Mr. Stewart's table at lunch. We're tracking down several other people. That's all I can say, but you can probably hold off on a call to the solicitors."

The mention of lawyers made me feel even worse as I thought of my mother entangled in the British legal system.

"That's good to know," Alex said, filling the gap in the conversation. "At least you have the security cameras from Parkview. You should be able to tell exactly what happened, right?"

Albertson shook his head, his craggy face shifting into dissatisfied lines. "The conservatory is too large. They weren't worried about theft in there. At Parkview, they put their money into monitoring the rooms and hallways with the high-end valuables."

"I suppose the urns and the massive statues would be hard to cart out of there discretely," Alex said.

Albertson gave a small grin. "Exactly. Only one camera covers the entire room. It's behind Mr. Stewart and at the other end of the room. It isn't powerful enough to record small details. We can only see the big picture."

"I'd forgotten about the cameras." A frisson of excitement went through me as my thoughts turned back to Nick. "You should be able to use the camera footage to trace Nick's movements on the night he died. You can tell exactly who he talked to and where he went, even who went outside, right?"

Albertson shook his head. "The tech is good, but not that good. We've been able to confirm his presence at one of the back tables for most of the event, except for a short period when he went to the loo then got lost on his way back. He wandered around the halls, stepped into a few rooms, but didn't meet anyone until an employee directed him back to the conservatory. The outdoor cameras only monitor the area immediately around

Parkview. We know he walked a young lady to her car. She was the last person to see him, apparently," Albertson said. "Don't spread that around. I know I can trust you to keep those details to yourself. And I know you two are always in the thick of things. Have you happened to run across anything we should know about?"

"Not about Malcolm," I said, "but I did hear that Nick may have been into drugs—marijuana."

Albertson ran his hand down either side of his mouth as he nodded. "Heard that from the folks at the inn, but we've seen no evidence of it."

"Really? I thought you would have found some trace of it in his suitcase or his car."

A man across the room caught Albertson's attention and waved. He said hurriedly as he began to move away, "Nothing like that in his belongings, and Davis used the bus to get around the village."

My mother's voice carried across the room. "See, I told you it was nothing to worry about." Several heads popped up and watched my mom as she crossed the room, her umbrella tapping out a counterpoint to her steps. She reached us and lowered her voice. "It was about poor Malcolm. Such a shame. You never can tell, even at nice places. You have to be so careful. That's why I never have chicken or tuna salad, which is a shame because I do like a good chicken salad."

"Malcolm didn't eat something that disagreed with him. He was poisoned. I told you that earlier on the phone," I said.

"Yes, I know, dear. So unfortunate for him. I'm only saying that it's a good idea to avoid certain things. They tend to spoil."

"Mom, that has nothing to do with—"

"Let's get out of here," Alex said, moving us toward the door and ending that conversation, a wise move on his part, I realized as I blew out a breath.

While we'd been inside the church hall, the storm had cleared out, leaving the sky a pearly blend of pink and orange as the sun dipped to the horizon. The streets were still damp from the rain, and the grass of the village green looked more vibrantly emerald than usual.

"Mom, I don't think you understand the seriousness of the situation with Malcolm."

"I understand it perfectly, Kate. Malcolm obviously crossed someone he shouldn't have—probably the same person who killed Nick. It's frightening to think about it. Who knew a little English village like this could contain so much violence—a knifing *and* a poisoning. The ladies at bridge will never believe me when I tell them about it."

"Mom, did it occur to you that Quimby might find it suspicious that you were with Malcolm right before he was poisoned?"

"Why should that matter?"

"He didn't act as if he suspected you might have something to do with it?"

"Me? What would I—oh, Kate. There you go again speculating and getting yourself all worked up. He only had a few questions for me. He wanted my *help*."

I turned away in frustration. I knew from long experience that I wouldn't be able to change her mind. Once Mom was set on an opinion, she didn't budge. Alex raised his eyebrows, conveying *do you want me to give it a shot?*

I shook my head and muttered under my breath, "It's no use. It's just wasted energy. She'll never believe us." Mom would go on in her own way, and I might as well give up trying to convince her she might be in danger either as a target of the murderer or as a person of interest in the investigation.

A double-decker bus pulled away from the village's bus stop, revealing Dad juggling several books and his phone. His head was down as he concentrated on his phone, but as soon as I called out to him from across the street, he looked up. He smiled and put away his phone as he trotted across the zebra crossing on the street, making it just before the light changed. "Hello, Kate. Alex."

I could tell from his upbeat tone that either he'd found more books, or he had some other news to share. He gave Mom a wary nod. "Ava."

"Oliver." She matched his reserve.

"Looks like it was a good shopping trip," I said to Dad in an effort to gloss over the tension between my parents.

"What?"

I pointed to the bundle he held. "The books."

"Oh, right." He looked at the stack as if he'd forgotten about them. "Yes, they had an impressive selection," he said quickly, as if it didn't matter. "I found out a few things about Nick. After I spoke to you—"

Alex cleared his throat and indicated something behind us.

"Sorry to interrupt," Quimby said as he strode up, his unbelted brown trench coat flapping with his swift pace. He stopped beside Mom. "One more thing, Mrs. Sharp. Please do not leave Nether Woodsmoor."

Mom stared at him a moment. "But that's not possible. I have an overnight trip to London scheduled for tomorrow."

Quimby's phone began to ring. "I'm afraid you have no choice. You'll have to reschedule. "

"But—"

"Sorry. No exceptions." He pressed his phone to his ear and walked back to the church hall, his raincoat beating against his legs.

"It's an all-day tour..." Mom called, but Quimby didn't turn back. She switched her attention to me. "He can't do that. He's treating me like some sort of criminal, telling me where I can and can't go. It's outrageous. I'll complain to...someone—someone at Parkview. They can set him straight."

"I'm afraid Quimby *can* do that," I said. "You were with Malcolm right before he was poisoned. I think you're actually

SARA ROSETT

lucky he let you leave after he questioned you. Did he ask for your passport?"

"No! That would be absurd," she said, but for the first time, I saw a shade of worry in her expression.

Dad rocked on his heels. "A poisoning. That's interesting."

"It's not interesting," Mom snapped. "It's tragic."

I refrained from pointing out that she only thought it was tragic after it affected her plans. Dad looked at his watch. "It's late. Has anyone eaten? If not, let's go somewhere, and I can tell you what I learned. Any good Indian places here? I want to try an authentic British Indian curry."

I glanced at Alex for his agreement that Indian food was okay with him then said, "Up the street and around the corner."

As we set off, Dad turned and called over his shoulder, "We'll be around the corner. Indian place."

The light still hadn't changed. The man who had sat so quietly not reading his newspaper in the pub this morning waited on the other side of the street with the rest of the bus passengers. When he realized Dad was speaking to him, he looked irked.

CHAPTER 21

"Me! Of all people," Mom said. "The thought that *I* would poison someone...have you ever heard anything so absurd?"

Dad murmured something under his breath, and Alex coughed hastily into his napkin. Mom ignored them both, but sent me a glance that clearly said, *men!* Then she continued, "I don't see why it matters that I had lunch with Malcolm." She pushed her half-full plate of Tandoori chicken away.

Mrs. Sandara brought us more naan. When we arrived she had been delighted to escort our group to a secluded table. At a word from Alex, she'd seated Dad's watchdog at a table near the front window on the opposite side of the room where he could barely see us. Dad had nodded his approval. While we waited for our food, Alex and I recapped our day, describing what we'd learned from Sylvia, Shannon, and Ella.

I reached for a piece of bread. "We've been over this Mom. You were the last person to be around Malcolm before he collapsed. It looks suspicious. And that's not even mentioning the feather at the crime scene."

"The whole situation is idiotic. I can't believe that the

inspector thinks I could stab someone. If I were going to kill someone, I'd find a better way to do it."

"Like poison?" Dad asked with a mischievous sparkle in his eye.

"Dad."

"Just a little joke to lighten the tension. I know you didn't do anything of the sort, Ava. That's why I asked around today about Nick. The police are obviously on the wrong track."

Mom shifted forward in her chair. "Speaking of asking around, why are you and Alex spending all your time running around asking people questions? Your father...well, he always did have rather odd interests so I'll let his activities go, but you two— you're on your *honeymoon*. You should be doing—er—honeymoon things."

"Mom, the police think either you—or you and Dad together—are good possibilities as prime suspects for Nick's murder."

"That's unbelievable. They can't *really* think—"

I tilted my head at the man at the front table. "Mr. Five-O'clock Shadow has followed Dad all day, and you've been questioned—twice. Then Quimby told you not to leave the village. The police don't do things like that on a whim."

"But that's...it's your honeymoon. You're taking time to do that...for me?"

"Yes," I said, surprised at her stunned expression. "For both you and Dad. You can't expect Alex and me to ignore Nick's death and jet off to Venice, leaving you and Dad at the center of the investigation. In fact, I don't know if they'd even let us leave at this point."

Dad pointed his fork at Mom's chicken. "Are you done with that?"

"I don't have an appetite anymore," she said, and I could see she realized the seriousness of the situation for the first time.

Dad picked up the plate and transferred the chicken to his

empty plate. "No use letting good food go to waste, even if you are upset."

Mom looked away from the pile of food. We fell silent as the waiter refilled our water glasses. Once the server departed, Mom took a long sip of water, then set it down and squared her shoulders. "I'm not sure talking to people will make any difference, but I know that I wasn't the only person near Malcolm's food today. Several people came to our table—a waiter to take our order, and then a different person actually served us our food. A different girl refilled our drinks. I told the inspector all of that."

"Quimby will check out everyone," Alex said.

"But does he know about that organist person? What was her name?" Mom looked at me.

"Sylvia? Sylvia was there?"

"A beautiful young woman with golden hair and a stunning figure, right?" At my nod, Mom said, "She came to ask Malcolm a question about a wedding that's scheduled for next week."

"Did she join you? Eat with you?" I asked.

"No, she apologized for interrupting, then asked her question. Something about which song the couple decided on. Then Malcolm introduced us, and she stood there a few minutes. We talked about how nice your wedding was. I didn't see her do anything to Malcolm's food, but I wasn't particularly watching. I suppose she could have dropped something onto his plate or put something in his glass. And the inspector doesn't even know about her. He only asked about why Malcolm and I ate together and what we ordered."

"The cameras." I looked at Alex.

He nodded. "They'll be able to see it on the footage. They probably already know." Alex explained to Mom about the video monitoring at Parkview.

"Well, I don't care if Parkview has a video. I'm calling Inspector Quimby now. Maybe he hasn't seen the recording yet. He gave me his card." Mom took out her phone. I thought she was probably looking forward to interrupting Quimby at whatever task he was focused on—a small revenge for her canceled sightseeing tour. Mom turned her back on us as she dialed then requested to speak to Quimby.

Dad touched his napkin to his lips and placed it beside his plate. "I took a detour on my way back today. Stopped off at two historic sites, Ridgeford Court and Aslet House."

"Dad," I said, my tone admonishing. "I don't like to think of you poking around on your own. It worries me."

"Oh, let your old dad have his fun. If you can snoop around, I can too. I had my shadow with me the whole time, so there was nothing to worry about. It will be interesting to see what the police make of my detour, if anything. I could have just had a hankering to see some historic Britain. Neither estate was far away from where I was. I took the train to both places and was able to walk to them—only a few miles each way."

He nudged his plate away and leaned forward so we could hear him over Mom insisting that it was urgent she speak to Quimby and that she would hold as long as necessary. "I found a news article with Nick's picture on my phone. I showed his photo around on the tours to see if any of the guides remembered him. No dice at the castle place, but I got lucky at Aslet House. I got the same guide Nick had. She remembered Nick well, said he was charming and had lots of questions."

"Questions about what?" I asked.

"Everything," Dad said with a snort. "Architecture, English history, irrigation methods, gardening, flowering plants, ghosts, urban foraging, tourism statistics, and—get this—fine china. I got the feeling that he was a question-a-minute tourist. She said she was exhausted when his tour was over. He did the whole thing, too. The house and gardens, as well."

"Did you do both tours?"

"Of course. I managed to get into the last slot of a departing tour, so my shadow had to wait for me," Dad said with obvious pleasure. He turned serious as he said, "I don't know that it helps us understand Nick any better, though."

"We know Nick lied all the time about his interests, so I don't think we can assume much from what he asked. Did the guide say if he had any specific questions?" I asked.

Dad rubbed his hand over his face. "I've been thinking about that all the way back here on the bus. The guide remembered a few specific questions. Nick wanted to know about ghosts and spirits connected with the house, about the engineering of the water features, about the famous people who had stayed there."

Mom slapped the phone down onto the table. "He said they were already aware of Sylvia. Imagine! Cutting me off from leaving Nether Woodsmoor when he has plenty of other people to investigate. Let him meddle with *their* schedules."

"He probably already has," I said.

Mom sniffed and said she was ready to go back to Parkview. She called Neal to pick her up, but Dad said he'd rather walk. We said goodnight outside the restaurant in deep twilight. As the Range Rover pulled away, Dad said, "You don't have to worry, Katie. I'll keep an eye on her."

"Thanks, Dad."

Alex offered him a ride back to Parkview, but he declined. "I need to stretch my legs after that bus ride." He set off along the path that would take him back to Parkview, and Alex and I headed for the church hall where the windows were still bright and the parking area was crowded with official cars. I was exhausted and glad to climb in the MG.

"Want to go anywhere else?" Alex asked.

I ran through all the questions I had, trying to think of anyone else who could shed some light on what had happened with Nick...or with Malcolm. "We haven't talked to Carl, but I can't come up with even a halfway reasonable excuse to show up on his doorstep and ask him if he knew Nick."

"We can stop by Parkview tomorrow and try to work it into

the conversation," Alex said. "I need to talk to him about extending our stay at Cart Cottage anyway."

"That's a much better plan than appearing at his house unannounced." I tipped my head back and rested it against the seat. We were both quiet as Alex drove through the narrow village lanes. As the last of the stone cottages disappeared behind us, the headlights picked out swaths of gently undulating countryside laced with dry-stone walls. I said, "Is it just me, or are things getting more confusing?"

"I'm right there with you," Alex said. "In fact, I've been confused from the beginning. Why would someone kill Nick? I still don't understand that."

"Other than the fact that it seems he was a compulsive liar and liked to blackmail people?"

Alex shot me a smile before returning his gaze to the dark road. "When you put it like that, it makes him sound like a good candidate for murder, but the only person we *know* he tried to blackmail was your mom, and..." He shook his head. "I don't see it. Your mother's journal...embarrassing, yes. Motivation for murder? No."

"But we know from Fern that he talked about coming into money," I said. "That could be another blackmail scheme—a scheme gone wrong since he's dead. But we haven't found anyone remotely connected to Nick who has a lot of money. Fern works as a paralegal and used her savings to pay for the trip here —so that doesn't sound like she's rolling in the dough. And Fern and Nick were engaged. He wouldn't blackmail his fiancée..." I lifted my head and shifted out of my lounging position as I rearranged some ideas. "*Could* he have been blackmailing Fern? We only heard her side of the story. We don't know anything about her, except her job. Maybe she comes from a wealthy family or has a trust fund or something. She could have something she wants to keep quiet from her family or employer."

"And she's the one who told you Nick mentioned big money."

"That's true. Sylvia said Nick mentioned an investment opportunity, but that didn't sound like a windfall like Fern described." Had Fern lied to me? What if Nick had never mentioned coming into money? What if Fern made that whole thing up?

We were silent a few moments, then Alex said, "Going back to possible blackmail targets, it doesn't sound like Sylvia would be a good candidate either. If she had a lot of money, I bet she would be going to auditions all day, not teaching music lessons and playing at weddings."

"She'd probably still be in California, but she was the last person to see Nick alive." At Alex's questioning glance, I added, "Albertson mentioned it when we were talking about the cameras."

"That's right, he did," Alex said.

"Sylvia said she left Parkview with Nick standing in the parking area, but she could be lying, too, I suppose."

"You mean she might have arranged to meet Nick later at the folly?" Alex tilted his head as he thought about it. "It's possible she drove out of sight of the monitoring cameras then parked along the road and walked to the folly."

"Someone must have set up a meeting with Nick at the folly. I don't think he decided on his own to wander around the grounds of Parkview at night and then hiked over to the folly—that's a long way…unless he got lost."

The lights on the dash illuminated Alex's brief smile. "From what Ella and Shannon said, he was prone to wandering, but I agree, the area around the folly and maze wouldn't be my choice for a nighttime stroll. It would be pitch dark out there. Only the gardens near the house are illuminated."

"And then you mix in someone poisoning Malcolm, and it just adds an extra layer of confusion," I said. "*Is* Malcolm's poisoning related to Nick's death somehow?"

"It would be quite a coincidence if it's not." Alex turned off the main road onto the asphalt lane to Cart Cottage. "An unrelated murder and a poisoning at Parkview within a few days of each other? I don't buy it."

"I don't either, but the methods are very different."

Alex said, "Maybe that was a strategic choice, an effort to make the incidents appear unrelated."

"If the same person killed Nick and then tried to poison Malcolm, we come back to the same question—why?" The car's headlights flashed over rich russet and blazing orange leaves that edged the lane. As I stared at the vibrant colors, I said, "I've been trying to think of a way that Nick and Malcolm were connected, and I don't have any ideas. Sylvia said they spoke briefly at the reception, but that doesn't seem like it would be long enough for any sort of significant exchange."

"A blackmail threat might not take that long to deliver."

"But then why did Nick want to get into the wedding? If he wanted to blackmail Malcolm, he could have asked Shannon to introduce them earlier this summer. In fact, she offered, and Nick turned her down." The arch of trees fell away, and Alex downshifted as we crossed the clearing to the parking area near the cottage's door. "You'd think that as we learned more, things would come into focus, but it's the opposite. Everything gets more blurry. Let's forget the whole thing for a little while."

"Excellent plan," Alex said.

$\sim$

I blinked and lay still in the bed. What had woken me? Was it the faint daylight? The pillow beside me was empty and the covers on Alex's side of the bed had been thrown back. I shifted around and squinted in the thready light penetrating through the bedroom's single small window. Almost dawn on a cloudy day. Maybe Alex couldn't get back to sleep and had gone downstairs to keep from waking me.

We'd spent the evening in front of a blazing fire. It was the best thing that had happened all day. When we'd gone upstairs to bed, I'd thought I would toss and turn all night. But my last memory was of curling up on Alex's shoulder.

I spotted a piece of paper propped up on the nightstand on Alex's side of the bed. It was an old receipt from the White Duck. I tilted the backside toward the window and read Alex's neat printing. "Can't sleep. Going for a walk. Will bring back breakfast."

A floorboard creaked downstairs, and I snuggled down into the sheets, drawing the blanket tighter around me. Alex was back, but there was no hurry to get up. The air had a definite coolness to it this morning. He'd turn up the heat. I'd let the cottage warm up before I got out of bed. Maybe he'd even make another fire, I thought as I felt my limbs relaxing in the warmth of the bed.

Distantly, I heard another footstep on the floorboards, then the snick of a match being struck. I shifted around so that I could see the stairs and waited for Alex to trot up quietly.

A metallic click sounded. I recognized it. It was the noise that had woken me. I knew with an instinctive certainty that it was the sound of the lock sliding home on the front door as it closed. We were probably out of firewood, and Alex had left to get more logs, which were stored in a covered shed on the side of the property.

I waited a few moments, listening for the click of the door lock fastening again, but the cottage was silent. When the silence continued, I tossed back the covers. I slipped into my robe and padded silently to the staircase. I don't know why I was so careful not to make a noise, except that I suddenly had an uneasy feeling.

I took a few cautious steps down the circular staircase, the metal cold on the soles of my feet. As I came around the twist that gave me a view of the main room, I stopped, stunned.

A fire burned in the grate, but the hearthrug was also ablaze. Little flames danced across the tight-coiled fabric of the rug.

I raced down the rest of the steps and grabbed a heavy blanket from across the back of the couch. I tossed it on top of the rug, praying that the blanket was thick enough to smother the flames. It seemed to work because the blanket didn't catch fire, but for good measure, I hurried into the kitchen, intending to pull the fresh flowers out of the vase and use the water to douse the hearthrug, but a wall of putrid air hit me.

I gasped, instinctively stepping back. My gaze shot to the two-burner cooktop where one knob was tilted to the side. The clicking sound that signaled that the gas was on finally penetrated my brain. I clapped my hand over my mouth and nose, trying to ignore the awful smell as I darted forward and flicked the knob to the OFF position.

I fumbled with the catch on the window over the sink and shoved it open. I yanked the vase off the table and tossed the flowers on the floor as I ran to the fireplace. The acrid smell of smoke was heavy in the air. The rug wasn't on fire or smoldering, so I tossed the water on the flames in the fireplace. It sizzled and smoked, but I didn't stay to see if the fire was out completely. I wrenched open the front door and collided with Alex.

CHAPTER 22

*A*lex's arms closed around me, and I pressed into him. "Kate—?"

"A fire—and gas. One of the burners on the stove was on." I realized I still held the vase, and it was pressed between us, the water drops on the outside of it soaking into my robe and Alex's jacket. "You didn't start a fire before you left this morning, did you?"

"No, of course not. I wouldn't want to leave it burning since I was going out."

He pushed back from me and ran his hands over my shoulders and arms then cupped my face. "You're okay?"

"Yes." I leaned against one of his hands for a moment.

He gave me one of his penetrating looks then nodded. "I'll be right back."

"Alex—" But he was already inside, moving swiftly from the living area to the kitchen. He checked behind the stove then opened another window in the living area before he returned to the porch.

"That was no accident." He gave me a tight hug. "Are you sure you're okay?"

I'd never seen his eyes look so dark. I put a hand on his chest and felt his heartbeat racing. "Yes. I'm not hurt. Now that you're out here, I'm fine."

"What happened?"

"I woke up and heard someone in the cottage. I thought it was you. I found your note and thought you'd come upstairs, but when you didn't climb the stairs I went down to find you."

He ran his hand over his mouth. "I didn't even go into the kitchen this morning on my way outside. There's no way I bumped that knob on the stove and turned it on as I left."

"And the fire..." I trailed off, suddenly feeling sick. Someone had been moving stealthily inside the cottage, building a fire, clicking on the gas, and then leaving quietly, closing the door with only a whisper of sound. I felt cold, and it had nothing to do with the chilly air that circulated around my bare feet.

Alex pulled off his coat and wrapped it around my shoulders. He took the vase from me and set it down on the porch then picked up a to-go cup that was sitting beside the door beside a crinkled paper bag. "Have a sip of this." He handed me the coffee then retrieved the bag. "Let's go over here." He indicated two wrought-iron chairs situated in the grass. "The smell of gas was faint when I went in, but let's give it a few more minutes."

The aroma of coffee wafted from the cup, and I sipped gratefully after I curled up in the chair, tucking my bare feet under the hem of my robe.

"I already had a cup this morning at the pub," Alex said, "but brought this one back for you, along with some food." He opened the bag, took out a squashed cranberry muffin, and broke off a piece for me. I shook my head, but he said, "Go ahead. You've had a shock. A little food is probably what you need. And I think we're going to be here a long time this morning. We shouldn't touch anything downstairs."

"You're right." I reached for the muffin, knowing we needed to call the police and report what had happened. After a few bites of muffin and sips of coffee, I said, "But we don't know anything —anything, at all. Why would someone do that? All we've done is talk to people. We don't have any answers."

Alex looked out across the little clearing to the dense growth of the trees. The sky had lightened to a grayish-blue, but the trees were still black. I could barely distinguish the faint outlines of the tree trunks from the low-growing plants that filled in around their bases. "Maybe we do," Alex said, still looking at the wall of darkness under the pale sky. "Maybe we just don't realize it."

Despite the warmth of Alex's coat and the coffee I held, I couldn't suppress a shiver.

We finished the muffin in silence, then Alex said, "I'll call the police. Why don't you change into something warmer?"

The frigid flagstones of the little porch made me hop quickly to the door, but I hesitated beside the front door, which we'd left open to help circulate the air. Inside the cottage, the gas odor had faded. The temperature had dropped as air swept in through the kitchen window and then out the front door, bringing with it an earthy, damp smell. The ground was saturated from yesterday's rain. The fire smoldered in the grate, sending out thin lines of smoke. With my hands buried in the pockets of my robe, I bent over and peered at the handle on the front door. Both it and the latch were shiny. Not a single scratch marred the lock, the door, or the doorframe.

My hands shook as I tossed the last of my clothes into my suit-case. I wasn't staying in Cart Cottage a moment longer. Someone had tried to end our honeymoon, our life—everything. I shoved my shoes on top of my clothes and zipped the suitcase. Normally, I could pack quickly and efficiently. Traveling light and moving rapidly were part of being a location scout, but I had thrown everything in the suitcase without bothering to fold or arrange

SARA ROSETT

anything. I'd worry about wrinkles later. Right now, I wanted out.

Alex carried my suitcase down the circular stairs, and I followed him slowly. The cottage itself still looked cozy and inviting, despite the lingering smoky smell and the mass of charred rug in front of the fire. Thank goodness for the hard-wood floors. If it had been carpet...I shut down those thoughts.

We'd closed the windows, which trapped the sooty smell inside. I crossed the room quickly, not wanting to linger. Alex and I had agreed that we should move somewhere less secluded. Going back to either of our cottages was not an option. Honey-suckle Cottage was no longer my cottage, and repair work was going on at Alex's cottage. I knew from all the wedding-planning discussion with Malcolm that Parkview's rooms were full, so I called Doug. He said he'd hold a room for us. After checking in, I would drop off the keys to Cart Cottage at Parkview. I'd already left a message for Carl to let him know what had happened. *If he didn't already know...* I pushed the thought away. Alex and I hadn't talked about who could have set the fire. We'd been too busy packing and contacting the police. I didn't want to think about it until I was away from the cottage.

Alex placed my suitcase into the trunk of the MG beside his. "I'll be there as soon as they finish here."

Constable Albertson had already examined the cottage and called for the crime scene investigators. He had told us that normally something like this would be handled on the local level, but since it might be linked to Nick's death, which was an ongoing investigation, the crime scene people would "have a look."

They were on their way and would take fingerprints and gather any other evidence they could find. I'd told Albertson all I could, which wasn't much. I'd heard the noises, thought it was Alex, and waited a few moments, then went down to check on things.

"Good thing you did," Albertson had said. "With the little red car still parked out front, the person who did this thought you were both asleep upstairs. It would have been quite early for honeymooners to be up and about." He had glanced at the thick growth of trees that enclosed the clearing around the cottage. "Lonely out here. Easy for someone to walk or even drive in without being seen. You didn't hear a car?"

"No, but I suppose they could have parked about halfway down the lane, and I wouldn't have seen or heard them. I didn't come downstairs right away."

"It's a shame it's an asphalt approach. Otherwise we might have been able to get some tire tracks."

Alex closed the trunk and handed me the keys to the MG. Albertson was currently examining the back and sides of the cottage for footprints. He'd checked the asphalt lane first and came back shaking his head.

I opened the door of the car. "You won't stay here by yourself?"

"Once they finish here, Albertson will give me a lift to the inn." Alex felt that one of us should stay at the cottage and make sure it was locked up after the crime scene techs left. Albertson could have handled it by himself, but I hadn't argued with Alex. I knew his years of location work were kicking in. Experience had taught both of us that it was smart to oversee things personally, especially the final shutdown of a location, which was what this situation was beginning to feel like.

I kissed Alex quickly. "I think I'll check on my mom this morning after I get our room. Make sure she didn't ignore Quimby and leave on her tour anyway," I said.

"Sounds like a good idea. Send me a text if you stay at Parkview. I'll ask Albertson to drop me there, if that's where you are."

The sun was bright now, and the rolling landscape sparkled in the morning sunlight. Splashes of gold, red, and copper leaves flickered along the road, but I couldn't concentrate on the change of season. Alex's words from earlier this morning echoed in my mind.

Did we know something, but didn't realize it? I pulled into the inn's parking lot and sat there a moment, running through everything that had happened. I could think of one person who was connected—or could be connected—to everything that had happened…well, almost everything, but I didn't have proof.

And then there was the question of why? Why would someone be desperate enough to commit murder? I turned off the car. I couldn't answer either question, and I needed more than speculation before I went to Quimby.

~

Doug took one look at me and shook his head in wordless sympathy. "You'll be safe here. No need to worry."

I hadn't given him any details when I called. I only told him we'd had a change of plan and asked if he had a spare room available. "Already? Really? How can you know what happened?" I asked. "That has to be a record, even for Nether Woodsmoor, if you know about the gas leak that fast."

"Constable Albertson's wife knows Marie's aunt, who mentioned it to Marie, who mentioned it to me," he said with a grin.

Some things—like village gossip spreading faster than a virus —never changed. I followed Doug, who had insisted on carrying the suitcases, upstairs to the room. As he left, I glanced around the antique furniture and chintz, feeling steadier in the familiar surroundings. I didn't bother to unpack, only checked that I had the keys to Cart Cottage and my phone, then went back downstairs again.

"Kate," Doug called as I crossed the entry area. "Almost forgot to give this to you."

He removed a large mailing envelope from the shelves behind the reception desk and handed it to me.

"What's this?" I didn't recognize the handwriting. "I didn't know you were the post now." My name was scrawled across the front, but there was no address under it. The return address area was also blank.

"Neither did I. A young woman blew in this morning and asked if I could see that you got it. Said it was important —*extremely* important." Doug imitated the last two words, pronouncing them in an American accent. "I told her you were on your way here. If she stuck around she could give it to you herself, but she didn't want to do that."

"Long dark hair?" I ran my finger along the envelope's seam. "Sort of dramatic?"

Doug opened a drawer and handed me a pair of scissors. "That was her. She left in a taxi."

I cut the envelope open and found a composition notebook inside. On the square in the center of the black-and-white marbled cover, a faded handwritten line read, *1985*. The edges were worn, and a large section of the marbled cover was missing on one upper corner, leaving the cardboard backing showing through in a diagonal shape.

A piece of paper stuck out of the top, so I opened the notebook to it. The thin napkin was similar to the one I'd used in the pub to jot down our questions. The ink from the pen had bled at some points, but it was readable.

Kate,

This diary belonged to Nick's mother, and he said it was worth a lot. Once I knew he'd lied to me about where he was traveling, I took it from his apartment. He thought I didn't know where he kept it, but under the mattress is like the worst hiding place ever! Since he'd never let me look at it, I wanted to see what the big deal was. Nothing! Just a bunch of

*boring stuff about traveling around. I kept reading, thinking that I'd
find the part that made it valuable, but—like I said—there's nothing
there. I suppose I should give it to the police, but now that they've said I
can leave, I'm not taking any chances. (I can finally get out of this
horrible, wet place.) You can give it to them for me! And if they don't
want it (and why would they?) you can give it to your mom. You said
she was into all the family history stuff, so she might like it.*

—Fern

CHAPTER 23

I tucked the note into the front of the composition notebook and flipped through the pages. Dates headed the entries, beginning with January first. The handwriting was easy to read. I skimmed a few paragraphs describing a city and a hotel. Other entries recounted conversations. A few doodles in the margin caught my eye. One captured the soaring clock tower of Big Ben in a few strokes while another showed two young men laughing over pints.

The phone on the reception desk rang, drawing me back to the present. I tucked the diary into the outer pocket at the back of my purse. I now understood that the diary was what caused Fern to give off her I've-got-a-secret vibe when I spoke to her at the top of the hill. She must have still been trying to figure out if it was valuable when I'd spoken to her. I was irritated that she'd dumped the diary on me. I'd have to call Quimby, but before I did that, I would run by Parkview.

I checked the time. The estate office at Parkview didn't open until nine, so I had plenty of time to check on Mom first. While I was waiting, I'd check out the diary.

~

"Of course, I'm here." Mom peered through the gap between her door and the doorframe. "Where else would I be with that inspector insisting I cancel my sightseeing trip?" The door inched open, and I could see she was wearing a robe with a blue paisley design. "Do you think I can get them—the police—to reimburse me for the day tour?"

"I doubt it. Do you want to have breakfast?"

"Now? It's barely eight."

"And if you were on your tour, you'd already be halfway to London, I bet."

One corner of her mouth turned up. "You're right. Give me a few minutes. I'll meet you in the conservatory. Order me a spinach-and-mushroom omelet."

It was a nice morning and the other guests were on the terrace, so the airy room was quiet. I ordered two omelets and fruit, then called Quimby. I left him a message about the diary. Albertson had said Quimby had been informed about the gas leak, so I didn't mention that. I also didn't say anything about my inkling about who killed Nick. I couldn't take an inkling to the police.

I took out the diary and skimmed it as I waited for breakfast. Many of the first entries were only the name of a city, usually somewhere in England, and a few lines, something like "small crowd, but into it," or "wasn't worth the time."

By spring, the numbers listed with each city were growing and the notation "sold out," appeared more and more. Then in the summer, one entry caught my eye. The writing was harder to read as if it had been scrawled quickly.

Tom finally believes me. I've known for months that Mike has been taking quite a lot off the top for himself, but Tom refused to believe it until he saw the actual merchandise receipts from the gig in York. Tom was furious of course, and rightly so. At last! Getting the actual receipts without Mike knowing was a headache, but if Tom finally understands what Mike has been up to, then it will be worth all the trouble. Now, at least Tom knows what we're dealing with.

I glanced over the entries that listed only locations and numbers. Interspersed with these numeric entries were a few long summaries of conversations—heated arguments, it sounded like, between Tom and Mike. A longer entry in August caught my eye.

It's done. We're done. It's over! Tom finally had it out with Mike last night. I'm so happy I could dance around the room—and I did, but not when Tom could see me. I understand how worried he is about going out on his own, but I know he'll do great.

Mike denied everything. Of course. I knew he would, but Tom had documents—well, I had documents. Mike couldn't talk his way out of it this time. Tom told Mike he won't go public—because of Helena—but that The Zeros were done. Tom is scared to death of course, worried that he won't be able to compose on his own, but I know he can do it. The tour is over. They've fulfilled the contract. Nothing ties them together anymore, thank goodness. I know it will—

"That's quite a good sketch of Town Hall in Manchester," the waitress said as she refilled my orange juice.

I'd been so caught up in the diary entry that I hadn't paid any attention to the sketch in the margin on the opposite page. Now I looked closely and saw that it wasn't Big Ben as I'd first thought. The clock tower did resemble the famous London landmark, but instead of an almost free-standing clock tower, this sketch showed a clock tower that rose from an ornate Victorian building.

"Here I am." Mom hooked her black umbrella over the back of

her chair. The waitress returned with our omelets and coffee for Mom.

I closed the diary and put it on the corner of the table.

"Why are you up so early?" Mom glanced around. "And where is Alex? You didn't have a fight, did you?" She asked her last question in a suspicious tone before she popped a bite of omelet into her mouth.

"No, nothing like that." My first instinct was to make up some excuse and gloss over what had happened at the cottage. That's what I usually did. I avoided telling her anything that would cause her to worry, telling myself that she was miles away, and she'd only work herself into a state. But she wasn't miles away. And she was as involved in the mess around Nick as I was—more involved actually, considering her lunch with Malcolm. I put down my fork. "I don't want to worry you—especially since everything is okay—but there was a little...um...incident this morning."

"Kate, you're scaring me. What happened?"

"There was a gas leak at the cottage." I recounted the whole thing, explaining about the leak and how someone started a fire in the fireplace. Then I said, "Alex and I decided to move to the inn."

"Oh, Kate." She set down her coffee. "This is getting worse and worse. Why didn't you and Alex come here?"

I was glad to see she didn't launch immediately into dramatic mode. At her core, Mom is a bit of a showman. Drama is her default setting. If things aren't thrilling or sensational enough she finds a way to make the situation dramatic. But now that we were facing something truly dire, she'd abandoned her usual theatrical manner. I said, "Parkview is booked."

She nudged her plate with the barely touched food to the side and leaned forward, elbows on the table. "It's one thing to have to answer questions from the police and then have them reorganize your schedule, but what happened to you—that's dangerous. We can't have that. We have to do something. Oh, I know you and Alex and your father are asking around, but that's not working. We have to do something else." She sat up straight. "My first choice is to leave, but I doubt that's going to happen. How long can it take the police to figure out what happened? Surely they can't keep us here indefinitely?"

"I think they can." I hurried on before she could protest again. "I have an idea—it might be completely off, but, well…it's all I have at this point. I don't see how it all fits together, but…here, take a look at this."

I handed her the diary, and she sent me a half-indulgent frown. "I don't think this is the time to read your old journals. How did you get this here? I thought all these were boxed up at the condo." She ran her hand over the diagonal section of exposed cardboard on the top corner.

"Mom, it's from 1985. Way before my time."

She focused on the inscription on the cover. "Oh. Then whose is it?"

"It belonged to Nick's mom. Take a look."

She removed a pair of glasses from her fanny pack-slash-money belt. She skimmed the first pages as I had done, then some text caught her eye, and she read more slowly. By the time the waitress removed our plates, Mom barely noticed as she turned the pages. She suddenly flipped to the front of the book and stared at the name on the inside of the cover. All I could make out from across the table was the capital *R* at the beginning of the name. "Rebecca…?" she murmured as she removed her glasses then her eyes widened. She slapped the diary down on the table. "He lied to me."

"Nick?" I asked.

"Yes. He told me he wasn't related to *that* Davis family. He even said his mom's name wasn't Rebecca."

"I'm not surprised. He lied to everyone."

"But the first time we met, I *specifically* asked him if his mother's name was Rebecca." She punched her glasses at me as she emphasized her words. "Tom Davis is such a common name, so that's why I asked about Rebecca. He flat-out *lied* to me."

"Well, if he didn't know you, I can almost see why he'd do it. You did say his dad's music was pretty popular."

"Oh, yes. The Edge of Zero songs—*Fatal Memory* and *Sure Feeling* and *Random Hello*—"

"Okay, I get it. They were popular."

"Still are. I hear their music all the time—piped in at the coffee shop and the grocery store, that sort of thing."

"Maybe he didn't want to deal with the notoriety if he told you he was related to the singer."

Mom huffed. "I wouldn't have behaved like a silly fangirl."

"What happened when he went out on his own? Tom, I mean? I didn't get that far in the diary."

"Rebecca wrote about the breakup of The Edge of Zero?" She put her glasses on and picked up the diary. "Where?"

"A little past the middle, I think."

Mom flipped pages, scanning as she went. "The breakup of the band was a huge deal at the time. Neither Tom nor Mike commented on it publicly, but everyone speculated about it. And the rumors, you wouldn't believe..."

She must have found the entry I'd been reading earlier because she trailed off into silence as she read down the page then quickly turned to the next entry.

While she read, my own thoughts were churning away. Finally, she looked up. "Mike? Sweet, shy Mike? He was *stealing?*"

"Looks like it," I said.

"But that doesn't sound like him. He was an orphan and seemed so happy to be part of a family—his music family, he called it. Oh, don't look at me like that. I watched an interview with the two of them, Tom and Mike. The interviewer played up the fact that they were opposites. Tom had a posh upper-class background, and Mike had nothing."

I wasn't interested in how the media had emphasized their differences years ago. I was more focused on what the diary meant in the present day. "I think the diary was Nick's leverage to get money out of Mike."

"What are you talking about?" She set down the diary and put her glasses on top of it. "I'm sorry. I'm still trying to adjust my mental picture of Mike—he seemed so *nice*."

"Maybe Nick didn't know why the group broke up until he got the diary from his mother's belongings. The timing fits with what Fern told me—that Nick began to talk about a new source of money after he cleared out his mother's things. And she said he checked everything—opened every box, read every scrap of paper. Maybe he was looking for something like this." I reached across the table and tapped the diary. "It fits Nick's pattern of behavior. He blackmailed you to get into the wedding. Why wouldn't he blackmail Mike so that the story of why the group broke up would stay a secret? Apparently, Tom didn't announce why they broke up because he didn't want to hurt Helena, whoever she was."

"She was Mike's wife. Their wedding was a big deal. They got married on an island in the Caribbean with paparazzi buzzing the ceremony in helicopters."

"So Tom didn't want to ruin *Mike's* career—he had a wife and maybe kids…?"

"No." Mom shook her head. "No kids. The marriage didn't last. A few years later they divorced. Again, it was big news. Why did you say *Mike* with that odd inflection?"

"I think it was a stage name. I think Mike is Malcolm."

CHAPTER 24

$\mathcal{A}$t Mom's incredulous look, I said, "What rock star is named Malcolm?"

She opened her mouth, then closed it. "You're right. It's not a rock-star-type name."

"No, it's not. And who else fits? Why was getting into the wedding so important to Nick that he'd blackmail you for an invitation? He must have wanted to speak to Malcolm. Maybe he'd tried to meet him, and Malcolm refused to see him. He turned down Shannon's offer to introduce him, but maybe that was because he'd already tried to approach Malcolm and been rejected. If Nick came here to Parkview, he could ambush Malcolm at a public event. You'd told him about how the wedding was taking place at this beautiful English country home."

"But how would Nick even know Malcolm worked at Parkview?"

"A blackmailer would find out everything he possibly could about his target, right? I bet he researched Malcolm online. In fact, I bet that's what the trip to Nether Woodsmoor was about

192

during the summer. Nick was checking things out, seeing what sort of life Malcolm lived."

"But how would Nick know where Malcolm lived? Or where he worked? If Malcolm used a stage name—and even Rebecca used the name Mike in the journal—then how would Nick know his name was really Malcolm?"

"I don't know," I said. "But he's the only one who fits. All Nick's other encounters that we've been tracking down were with women. Malcolm is the only person at Parkview who is the right gender and age to have been part of The Edge of Zero band." Except for Carl. Were Carl and Malcolm the same age? Malcolm with his sweater vests stretched over his paunch and his disappearing hairline seemed so much older than Carl, who was fit and lean, but pounds aged you. "Wait—the sketch!" I picked up the diary, and Mom caught her glasses as they slid off the cover. I found the page with the drawing of the two men.

"I didn't see this," Mom said. "I didn't get this far. That's a good likeness of Tom and Mike."

"Yes, but imagine Mike without that full head of wavy hair. What if he had a lot less hair and it was wiry more than curly?" I put my thumb over the curls. Mom squinted and tilted her head then said in a wondering tone, "It does look like Malcolm. Imagine...Mike here at Parkview. I even danced with him!"

"Don't get starstruck now," I said. "I think he's a murderer."

Mom glanced around the conservatory, which was still mostly empty. She lowered her voice. "You think *Malcolm* killed Nick?"

"It makes sense, if you think about it. Nick arrives, tells Malcolm to pay up or he'll announce the real reason The Edge of Zero band broke up. Nick even has written proof of what happened, his mother's diary. It sounds like a story that the tabloids would eat up." I gestured at her. "Look at your reaction to the diary. You couldn't wait to find out the story behind the band's breakup. Nick probably saw dollar signs from Malcolm. Or if Malcolm didn't come through, who knows what the tabloids would pay for exclusive interviews with Nick and the rights to print the diary. He might have even gotten a book deal out of it."

"But to kill Nick?" Mom asked in a whisper.

"You were worried about Nick coming back to demand more from you, and your secret wasn't that big. Imagine you'd left The Edge of Zeros behind, but their music is still popular. People recognize the songs and enjoy them. Questions linger about what happened. It could blow up fast. And then where would Malcolm be? Probably out of a job," I said. "If Ella's right and Malcolm is skimming money from Parkview, he wouldn't want any questions coming up about his dishonesty in the past. Any investigation or questions could uncover what he's doing now."

Mom shook her head. "I just can't picture it. He seems so...fussy."

"Then think about the rest of it." I put into words the thoughts that had been skittering around my mind since this morning. "Malcolm is tall and, for all his finicky ways, I think he'd have the strength to move Nick's body from the folly to the center of the maze. He works here at Parkview and has access to your room. He could get inside and get something distinct—a feather from your hat—and place it with Nick's body, so that when it was discovered you'd be linked to the crime. He was at the pub and must have overheard your argument with Nick the night before the wedding and figured you'd be a good distraction for the police to focus on instead of him. You left on your tour the morning after the wedding. Malcolm had plenty of time to go to your room and get the feather. If anyone saw him, he could say he was handling a special request for you. You tend to have a lot of those," I said.

"No more than the average guest, I'm sure."

I raised my eyebrow.

She ignored me. "Let me see your phone." I handed it over. "I hate these tiny screens," she said, but seemed to find what she wanted because in a moment she looked up and briefly held up the screen so I could see a Wikipedia entry for The Edge of Zero band. "Let's see..." She scrolled down the page. "Here it is. Mike Douglas Stewart," she read, "Born Malcolm Douglas Stewart." She made a tsking sound and handed the phone back. "It's right there on the Internet for anyone to find. And at the end it mentions Nether Woodsmoor."

"Nice," I said, impressed.

"Genealogy research has taught me that almost everything you want to find is on the Internet. This uncovering tidbits and putting them together is a lot of fun. It's actually quite similar to tracing a family tree. I can see why you like it. Don't give me that innocent look. Neal told me all about those other investigations."

"He probably thinks I'm a nosey American, doesn't he?" I asked. It was better to focus on Neal. I didn't want to dwell on the fact that I'd been glossing over some significant stuff in my life with my mom.

"Not at all. 'Clever girl,' he called you."

"That's nice of him," I said. I wasn't always sure how the villagers felt about me. Louise was a friend, and I knew where I stood with her, but some of the other villagers had a reserved manner, and it was hard to read them. "But I'm not clever enough to figure this out completely. One thing doesn't fit—the gas leak."

"What do you mean?"

"Malcolm couldn't have done it. He's in the hospital. And someone poisoned him. Who did that?"

"An accomplice?" Mom asked. "The person turned on him and then tried to set fire to your honeymoon cottage?" she said in a questioning voice as she tried out the theory.

"But who could that be?" I asked. "I don't think Malcolm has any good friends." But I wasn't sure. My only interactions with him had been at the Parkview estate office. "I've seen him at the pub occasionally, but he was always alone. Ella might know who he is close to." I tucked the diary into the outer pocket of my purse as the waitress brought the check.

Mom signed to put the meal on her room. "I wasn't finished reading the diary."

"It's too valuable for us to be flashing it around." I was glad that most of the guests were on the terrace. Except for our waitress, who was moving away through the tables back to the kitchen, the only other occupant of the conservatory was a woman on the far side of the room who was feeding bites to the Pekinese she held in her lap.

I checked the time. "I have to go by the estate office on my way out. It will be open now. I'll ask Ella who Malcolm is friendly with." I'd also ask Ella if she knew who had access to the keys to Cart Cottage, but didn't mention that to Mom. She had taken the news about the gas leak much better than I'd expected, but I wanted to avoid bringing up the topic again.

Mom pushed back her chair. "I'll come with you."

"You don't have to do that."

"I'm not letting you run around alone with that diary. You said yourself it's valuable. Just let me get my jacket from my room." She picked up her umbrella.

"Where's Dad this morning? Do you know?" I asked as we left the conservatory.

"I have no idea. Probably tramping around outside since it's not raining at the moment. If he's not out, he's holed up in the library." We reached the foot of the stairs in the entry hall, and she said, "I'll meet you in the estate office."

"It's a nice day. I don't think you'll need a jacket."

"This is England, Kate. You *always* need a jacket and an umbrella."

I went down the corridor to the estate office. I noticed the tapestry that Malcolm had pulled down had been removed. The exposed section of the wall looked blank despite the elaborate molding and trim. Oil paintings, tapestries, and display cases filled every inch of the rest of the wall space.

Carl came barreling out of the estate office as I approached. I stepped back so we didn't bump into each other. "Carl, I have the keys—"

"Sorry, Kate. I can't speak to you at the moment. Minor crisis below stairs. Ella can help you with anything you need," he called over his shoulder. "She'll be back in a moment."

He obviously hadn't listened to his messages yet. The office was unlocked, but empty. It was a few minutes before nine, and I was sure Ella or someone else would be here soon. I headed to Carl's desk, intending to leave the keys and a note, but the squeak of a desk chair drew my attention to the back of the room.

A computer monitor blocked the person from my view for a moment, but then he shifted. I saw the familiar tweed jacket over a sweater vest. My stomach flipped. "Malcolm." I managed not to add, *what are you doing here?*

"Kate." He stood so abruptly that his chair shot out behind him and banged against the cabinet in the alcove with the sink and refrigerator. He held a half-empty glass of the green smoothie he liked so much in his hand.

My heart began to pound. The momentary look of astounded shock that passed over his features told me everything I needed to know. He hadn't expected to see me any more than I'd expected to see him. He'd thought I was still in the cottage.

I swallowed. "You're feeling better, then?" I made an effort to even out my words, hoping they didn't sound choppy like my breathing. "I thought you were still in the hospital." I'd stopped walking when he shot up out of his chair, so now I was stranded in the center of the room, a maze of desks surrounding me.

I eased back a step, my thoughts flying. I wanted to get out of the room, away from Malcolm, but if I raced out of here, he'd definitely know something was wrong. And where was Mom? I couldn't leave without her. She was meeting me here. I couldn't sprint to the car without her. No, better to stay calm instead of bolting. Ella would walk in soon, or Carl would return. Malcolm couldn't do anything here. With his padded figure and fuzz of receding hair, he didn't look threatening. In fact, it was hard to imagine him plunging a knife into Nick's chest. It was hard to imagine him even considering doing something like that. He might get a spot on his sweater vest and, besides, it wasn't the "done thing." My breathing smoothed out. I had nothing to worry about here in an office on a bright weekday morning. As soon as Mom arrived, I'd make some excuse and hustle us out the door.

"I insisted on being released this morning." He lifted the shake. "Pure living—that's what I need. Not pills and IV drips." He seemed to focus on something to the side of me, then he blinked rapidly. "Let me get you some."

"No, thank you. I just finished break—"

"I insist. It won't take a second to whip up one of these." He set down the glass and turned to the alcove, but paused for a second, his hands resting on the counter, his chin tucked down to his chest.

"Are you okay?" I asked.

"Perfectly...fine." He took a breath between the words. He gave his head a little shake then swung open the door of the small refrigerator. He removed several plastic bags, all filled with leafy green things, and placed them on a wooden cutting board. He held up one bag. "Kale, the base. It's essential." He half-turned to me, and I saw a thin line of perspiration had broken out across his high forehead. "Have a seat." He gestured at the chair by his desk, then rubbed his eyes before taking out another bag. "Must have spinach, too. Please, sit. I only use organic ingredients."

"No, thanks. I can't stay. In fact, I'm meeting my mom..." My gaze pinged back and forth between the green smoothie and the bags of kale and spinach. The plastic bag, the tours, getting "turned around" inside Parkview—it all made sense. I'd been wrong. Nick hadn't come to Parkview to blackmail Malcolm.

"Won't take a second...oh, look." He held up the blender. "I have some left. I didn't realize. Have a taste." He abandoned the piles of frilly green leaves on the cutting board and poured what had been left in the blender into a clean glass that he took from the draining board by the sink.

He came across the room toward me, his steps weaving. "Give it...a...dry—I mean, try. Quite...testy. No, *tasty*."

I backed toward the door, bumped into a desk, and moved around it. "No, it's poisoned."

He stopped, swayed, and I thought for a second he was about to collapse, but he remained upright. He brought the glass up to the level of his eyes and peered at the thick green drink then shook his head in an exaggerated way. "No. It wasn't this. *I* made this. It was launch—*lunch,* I mean—that was poisoned." His face suddenly convulsed into a grimace. He dropped the glass, and, in a blur of motion, lunged at me.

At the same moment, I heard a step behind me, then a *whoosh*. A wall of black exploded in front of me, cutting off my vision. A thin silver blade pierced the blackness and sliced downward. A tweed covered arm held the knife as it descended.

I jerked backward, bumping into Mom. We stumbled back a few steps, thumped into a desk, then skittered to the side, our arms and the umbrella tangled. Once the umbrella was out of the way, my gaze fixed on Malcolm. I expected him to surge up for another strike with the knife.

But he stayed on the floor. I wasn't sure if he had passed out or had hit his head on the way down and had knocked himself unconscious. Either way, I was glad he wasn't moving and that the knife had slid out of his reach under a desk.

"There, you see," Mom said in a breathy voice. "An umbrella is *always* a good idea in England."

CHAPTER 25

"*A*nd it was his smoothies that were poisoned all along."
Mom picked up a scone. "I *knew* it wasn't the food at lunch. Such a fuss for nothing."

"You can't blame the police for investigating," Dad said from across the table. "Malcolm's symptoms indicated an overdose of that heart drug, and it acts on the system quickly, so of course they assumed he'd ingested it at lunch. They didn't have time to get the tox screens back to know exactly what he'd ingested."

"But they were wrong about the heart drug." Mom added strawberry jam to her scone. "What was it again, Kate?"

"Hmm?" I shifted my attention away from Alex, who stood at the stone balustrade of Parkview's terrace as he spoke on his phone, his back to our table. It was the last morning we'd have together. Mom, Dad, Alex, and I were having breakfast before Alex and I—hopefully—departed. Our bags were packed and waiting at the side of the terrace. All we needed were the updated airline reservations, and we'd be on our way. The day was clear, but cool with a thin trace of clouds at the margin of the sky. I focused on Mom. "What did you say?"

"The poison, what was it?" Mom asked.

"Baneberry." Quimby had stopped by the inn last night and given Alex and me an update on the investigation. "Its symptoms are similar to a digitalis overdose—nausea, vision changes, convulsions, and shock—but the difference is that with baneberry, the symptoms may not show up for several hours or even several days, which is what Nick counted on."

"It was a berry?" Mom said. "I thought you said Malcolm only put spinach and kale and things like that in his drink? Wouldn't he have noticed some berries?"

"Baneberry does produce berries, and they have the highest concentration of poison, but the whole plant is poisonous. The leaves have a sawtooth pattern that's similar to marijuana leaves. What Marie thought was a bag of weed was actually a bag of baneberry. After Nick mixed the baneberry into Malcolm's smoothie ingredients, Malcolm didn't notice the slightly different leaves."

Dad, having finished his full English breakfast, including beans and tomatoes, inched his chair away from the table and crossed one leg over the other. "I've only heard bits and pieces about this. You said that baneberry was the reason Nick went on the stately home tours?" He picked up his cup of coffee and settled back in his chair. "I'd like to hear the whole story, please."

"Yes, that's what Quimby said. Shannon had told Nick about Malcolm's smoothies, so Nick already knew that Malcolm drank them and no one else did. Nick's next step was to find something to add to the ingredients that Malcolm kept in the small refrigerator in the estate office. Nick visited several sites in Sheffield then went to some historic homes and asked all sorts of questions to camouflage his real interest—baneberry. I looked up Aslet House's website. They offer specialized tours geared to different interests—textile tours for sewing and knitting enthusiasts, behind the scenes tours that take architecture fans into the attics and basement, and even "Experience History" tours that let guests dress in period costumes." A similar first-hand experiential event that I'd attended at Parkview had been interrupted by murder. My mother drew a breath, and I hurried on, thinking that Neal must have mentioned the incident when he described my run-ins with the police. "One of the garden tours at Aslet House is about urban foraging."

"What is that?" Mom asked, distracted.

"It's searching for edible food in urban environments, things like berries, mushrooms, nuts, and greens."

Mom looked at me a long moment. "Why wouldn't someone just go to the supermarket?"

"I guess urban foragers like the idea of finding food in the wild," I said. "Anyway, the area around Aslet House is, like Nether Woodsmoor, great for foraging with its hedgerows and woodlands. Lots of berries and nuts. They cover all of those details in the garden tour as well as which plants to avoid, like baneberry. It's all mentioned on Aslet House's website. I bet the investigators will find that Nick visited their website and read up on the urban foraging tour before he even left the States. He must have pocketed some of the baneberry during the tour and brought it to Nether Woodsmoor."

I turned to Dad. "You must have jogged the tour guide's memory. The next day she went to the police to report that the young man on her tour had seemed unusually interested in poisonous plants. Quimby told me that the woman said the more she thought about it after speaking to you, the more worried she became. She realized how many questions Nick had asked about dangerous plants. Apparently, he'd interspersed them with other questions so it didn't stand out at the time, but when she thought over it again, it worried her."

"I have to hand it to him," Dad said. "Nick's plan was ingenious. He arrived in England, learned about poisonous plants located here, collected some of them, then put them in Malcolm's ingredients. He didn't have a murder weapon in his possession to dispose of, and he'd be out of the country by the time Malcolm ingested the poison."

"And with Malcolm so interested in clean living and eating unprocessed foods, the police might have thought Malcolm had gathered the baneberry himself and eaten it, not knowing it was poisonous," I added.

"But how did you make the connection between the urban foraging business and Malcolm's smoothies?" Dad asked.

"I wouldn't have, if you hadn't checked on Nick's tours and told us about them. When Malcolm took out the plastic bags of kale and spinach to make a smoothie, I thought of Marie's description of the baggie in Nick's room. Everyone assured me that Nick wasn't into drugs, but what else could be in the plastic bag? It was only when I saw Malcolm's ingredients that I remembered you mentioned Nick's interest about urban foraging. That thought combined with the sight of all those baggies of chopped up leafy green things—well…," I shrugged. "The thought popped into my head, *What if the baggie Marie saw wasn't drugs?*"

I ran my hand along the edge of the table, remembering how my thoughts had raced along, but my feet had seemed to be bolted to the floor. If I was right that Malcolm had killed Nick, I'd been afraid to turn my back on him. I was pretty sure I'd spotted a knife in the silverware holder of the draining board, but if I was mistaken, then there was probably a knife in the drawer by the sink.

I shifted in my chair, reminding myself that I wasn't stuck in a room alone with Malcolm. I was in the sunshine and surrounded by my family. "Once my mind was running down that track, I wondered if Nick put something in Malcolm's food. Maybe Nick got lost on purpose and went to the estate office where he mixed his bag of baneberry into Malcolm's smoothie ingredients. The police found a small plastic bag with a few fragments of baneberry leaves in one of the trash bins in the estate office. Nick's fingerprints were on the plastic bag. I think Ella surprised

Nick, when she came into the office for her sweater, and Nick dropped the bag into the nearest trash bin so that she wouldn't see it. He had no choice but to walk out with her when Ella told him she'd take him back to the conservatory. I'm sure he hoped that the trash would be removed that night or the next day before Malcolm became ill."

"So his intention was to kill Malcolm all along," Mom said.

"It looks that way," I said. "Quimby said they found emails from Nick asking Malcolm to agree to license The Zero's songs for use in commercials and movies. They'd had several offers, but Malcolm had turned down each one. He refused to even discuss it. They held the ownership to the copyrights and the musical compositions jointly because Nick had inherited control of his dad's copyright and compositions. Nick couldn't sell or license the songs unless Malcolm agreed."

"If Malcolm needed money, why would he say no to a deal like that?" Mom asked. "I heard from the maid who does my room that they've called in an accountant who is reviewing everything Malcolm handled."

"Ella says they know now that Malcolm was taking money," I said. "In Malcolm's email replies to Nick, Malcolm said he wanted the band's music to stay pure, and that letting it be used in commercials would be wrong." I toyed with my fork. "I don't really buy that, though. I have to wonder if he sensed that Nick was a bit of a player and didn't want to get involved in any deals with him."

"You'd think one conman would recognize another," Dad said. "That's probably one reason he avoided the licensing deals. And there was the fact that Malcolm wouldn't want the past stirred up again. He seemed to like his anonymity here. Perhaps he worried that renewed interest in the songs might mean more questions about the band's breakup, which could only make him nervous."

"Nick must have decided blackmail was the way to go since Malcolm wasn't budging on the licensing deals," I said. "I think

Nick told Malcolm about the diary and said he would expose Malcolm's past shady activity if he didn't agree to license the songs, but Malcolm must have refused again—and that must have been when Nick decided to poison Malcolm. Since Malcolm had no heirs, Nick thought he'd be the sole owner of the songs. Without Malcolm around he'd have complete control over the licensing deals, which would be much more lucrative than any publicity he'd get from revealing the true reason The Zeros broke up."

"So he really did research Malcolm?" Mom asked. "That was why he traveled here earlier this summer?"

"Yes, he visited Nether Woodsmoor and researched Malcolm's work habits and environment," I said. "He knew from his conversations with Shannon that Malcolm had a smoothie every day and that no one else drank them or used the blender. He blackmailed Mom to get an invitation to the wedding. Remember how you said his writing was almost unreadable?"

"I could hardly make it out."

"Right," I said. "I'm sure it was on purpose. He couldn't ask for an invitation addressed to himself—that might tip off Malcolm, but with his bad penmanship he got an invitation addressed to a Mr. Mick David, which would let him get into Parkview without drawing too much attention to himself. He figured he could slip away from the event and plant the poison at a time when the estate office would be empty."

Dad said, "If anyone questioned him about the name variation on his invitation he could say they were typos."

"And it wasn't like they were checking IDs at the gate," I added. "Nick only needed an invitation and his name—or something similar to his name—on the guest list to get inside. Once he was on the grounds of Parkview he had the camouflage of nearly two hundred guests. Nick popped the baneberry in the refrigerator during the reception, knowing that when Malcolm made a smoothie on Monday morning, he would already be back in the States."

"He didn't count on Malcolm spotting him among the guests —or that Malcolm would fight back that night," Dad said.

"You'll be interested to know, Dad, that Malcolm's shoe size is the same as yours. Quimby says the dress shoes Malcolm wore the day of the wedding match the footprint left at the folly perfectly."

"So it was bad luck for me that I wore the same size," Dad said.

"But it was a lucky break for Malcolm. He'd already planted the feather from Mom's hat. With his job in the estate office, he could easily access guest rooms. But I'm sure he didn't mean to leave a footprint where the murder took place. The fact that the footprint was the same size as yours and caused the police to focus on you and Mom...well, it couldn't have worked out better for Malcolm."

Mom said, "Why did Nick go to the folly in the first place?"

"That's one thing Quimby wasn't sure about," I said. "Nick might have accidentally taken a wrong turn on his walk back to the village, which is possible because the path divides. One path takes you over the fields and back to the inn, but the other path curves back toward Parkview and the area by the maze and the folly. Or, Malcolm got Nick out to the folly somehow. If that's the case, then it must have happened when Malcolm and Nick talked briefly at the reception."

"But why would Nick do that?" Mom asked. "If Nick had already planted the poison why would he meet with Malcolm?"

Dad said promptly, "Because he had to string Malcolm along for another few days. If Nick suddenly lost interest in manipulating him, Malcolm might begin to wonder what had changed. Nick didn't want to do anything that would spook Malcolm or cause him to change his routine."

"Right," I said. "So Nick arrived at the folly either after accidentally taking a wrong turn or intentionally to play-act through a negotiation, not realizing Malcolm would be waiting with a knife."

"To think that I felt a teeny bit sorry for him when he was out cold on the floor." Mom shivered. "And that was the *second* time he tried to kill you, Kate."

Malcolm had ingested a larger amount of the baneberry the second time. With his system already weakened from the first bout with the poison, the impact of the second dose hit him much harder. I drew my jacket tighter around me. We were all silent for a moment. Malcolm hadn't been able to check himself out of the hospital this time. He'd never become fully coherent and had died during the night.

Mom cleared her throat. "Tell them about Nick's phone, Kate," she said. "You asked about that, didn't you?"

"Yes. Quimby told me they received the phone records from Nick's old phone," I said. "The phone they recovered from the lake didn't have any data on it related to Malcolm, but Nick had an older cell phone. They found it when they got Malcolm's phone records. Apparently, Nick bought a cheap cell phone and only used it to contact Malcolm. Nick sent Malcolm photos of the diary and some individual diary entries through that phone. He'd have to show Malcolm something to prove he had the diary. He got rid of the cheap phone, but the records of the texts and photos were still in the database of Malcolm's phone provider even though Malcolm had deleted the images from his phone."

I glanced at Alex, who had ended his call.

Mom said, "But I still don't see why Malcolm tried to set the cottage on fire."

"Alex was right," I said as he sat down beside me. I slipped my hand into his. "Alex and I *did* know something that we didn't realize was important. We worked it out yesterday."

Alex said, "Malcolm lied to Kate. When Kate asked him what he and Nick had talked about at the reception, Malcolm said

Nick complained about his car being blocked in, but Nick didn't have a car."

"He arrived on the bus and walked everywhere around Nether Woodsmoor," I said. "Constable Albertson even told us that, but I thought he meant that once Nick was here, he'd taken the bus instead of driving around the village. What he meant was that Nick didn't have a car, *at all*. Malcolm learned that Nick didn't have a car, and he realized he'd slipped up. He discharged himself from the hospital and came back here to pick up an extra key to Cart Cottage from Carl's desk. The police have the footage from the cameras recording his arrival here early that morning. Malcolm went to Cart Cottage, thinking that he could quietly set the fire and turn on the gas while we were still sleeping."

"But he wouldn't have an alibi for that," Dad said. "And if anyone checked the video recordings they'd see him taking the key."

I said, "The estate office doesn't have video monitoring. Cameras only record the corridors and the rooms with expensive items, so there wouldn't be a recording of Malcolm taking the key from Carl's desk. I'm sure he could have come up with an excuse for stopping at Parkview's estate office early if he was questioned—maybe that he forgot something essential or had a small task that had to be done before everyone got to work that morning. At that point, I think he was less worried about an alibi. He simply wanted us out of the way."

Dad swung his foot and stared out over the green expanse of the lawn to the belt of autumn-tinged trees. "So Nick wanted sole control of the songs, and Malcolm wanted to keep Nick quiet. Malcolm saw Nick was a threat and killed him, but Nick had already set up the poison that would kill Malcolm. A killing from beyond the grave," Dad said.

"Two murderers who murdered each other. If anyone ever deserved each other, it was those two." Mom propped her elbows on the edge of the table and looked over the rim of her coffee cup. Her eyes narrowed. "I wonder who gets the songs now?"

Dad laughed, a sharp bark. "Trust you to follow the money."

"Well, it's important. Those songs are what caused this whole mess."

"I'll never listen to the Muzak version of *Fatal Memory* the same way," Dad said, his tone dry. "If Nick didn't have a will and didn't have any siblings, then I suppose the rights would go to his parents, but you said they're deceased?" Mom nodded. "Any brothers or sisters?" Dad asked.

"Yes, Rebecca had a brother." Mom squinted at the sky. "I can't remember his name, though. He works in some sort of charity, I think. Orphanages in South America? I can't remember. I contacted his office when I was researching the family tree, but he was out of the country. Or maybe it was South Africa. Oh, I wish I could remember his name," Mom said. "That will bother me all day."

"I'm sure the police or lawyers will track him down, if you can't find him on your genealogical chart," Dad said. "And perhaps the money from the songs—if they are ever licensed or sold or whatever it is that happens with that sort of thing—will go to a good cause since it sounds like the brother will get the rights."

"Speaking of genealogy..." Mom put down her coffee cup and checked her watch. "I'm off to see that historic home in London. It belonged to one of our relatives. You remember, Kate. I told you about her, the high society detective..."

Dad didn't bother to suppress a groan. I exchanged an amused glance with Alex as he handed me a piece of paper. He'd written a flight number and departure time on it. "This afternoon," he said. "We're on the flight."

It was going to happen. We were going on our honeymoon. I smiled at him and tuned out the bickering between my parents. "I'm so glad."

SARA ROSETT

Our waitress approached with a long rectangular box.

"Good, it arrived." Dad reached for the box. Mom frowned at him as he set it across the arms of her chair. "No need to look so suspicious. I thought you might need it. Go on, open it."

Alex lifted an eyebrow at me. I shook my head. "No idea." The box was the right size for long-stemmed roses, but I doubted my dad would send those to my mom.

Mom put her coffee down and sent Dad a suspicious look before she used a knife from the table to cut the tape. She folded the flaps back and laughed. "You're right. I do need another one."

She pulled out a black umbrella as long as her arm with a glossy wooden handle. The sun glinted on the lethal-looking tip.

"Since the last one came in so handy..." Dad mumbled.

"Thank you, Oliver," Mom said, sounding sincerely pleased.

Dad shrugged, but I could see he was glad she was happy. "Just watch yourself with it," he said. "No poking people in the back or that sort of thing."

"Oh, Oliver. Why do you always have to ruin a nice moment? It's just like you..."

I turned in my seat so that I was angled toward Alex. "I thought for a moment there they were going sentimental."

"No need to worry about that," Alex said as their sparring continued.

"I have to do one more thing before we leave. Download a book that Grace recommended."

Alex said, "A murder mystery, I bet."

"Yes," I admitted. *Busman's Honeymoon*, a Lord Peter book, but don't worry. During our honeymoon, any mystery or mayhem will be strictly between the pages of a book."

"Excellent. We'd better say our goodbyes and get going." Alex shifted his chair back then paused before he stood. "We have one small modification to the itinerary. We change planes in Paris, but the rest of the flights to Venice are booked. I'm afraid we have to take the train, and it's not the most updated equipment. Kind of old, in fact." One corner of his mouth quirked upward. "But I think you might like it. It's called the *Orient Express.*"

"You're kidding." I searched his face for a hint that he was joking.

But he wasn't teasing. He smiled widely. "Nope. I'm serious. It will be two separate berths, no shower, and a bath shared with something like ten other people in our carriage, if we want to get to Venice. Food's supposed to be excellent, though."

"Sounds perfect."

THE END

THE STORY BEHIND THE STORY

Thanks for reading Kate and Alex's latest adventure. I had a wonderful time visiting Nether Woodsmoor again and crafting a mystery with double murderers.

Like Kate's mom, I found the genealogy aspect of this story fascinating. A spin-off series, set in 1920s England is in the works. If you're interested in news about the High Society Detective series, let me know at SaraRosett.com/1920s. I'll drop you a line when the first book is out.

Writing *Death at an English Wedding* was a bit daunting. So many fun characters are part of the series. I wanted to include them all, but many of my favorites only got a passing mention or a cameo because the focus had to be on Kate's family for this book. My own parents are nothing like Ava and Oliver, by the way. They are happily married and never tried to set me up on a blind date. (Thank goodness.)

When I first had the idea for this series, I knew Jane Austen themes would be part of it. Kate and Alex's family and friends pushed Jane almost completely out of the story this time, but she will be back. *Pride and Prejudice* plays a big part in the plot of the first book in the series, *Death in the English Countryside*. When I was knocking ideas around for that book, I thought *what if Kate's parents were modern day versions of Mr. and Mrs. Bennet?* What would they be like today? From that jumping off point, I decided they'd be divorced, no question about that. Kate's dad would still be into books—so much so that he owns a bookshop. And Kate's mom would be obsessed with marrying Kate off and continually ambushing her with blind dates. From those initial ideas, Ava and Oliver came to life. In this book, I enjoyed exploring their relationship with Kate and with each other. On second thought, I guess *Death at an English Wedding* does have some Jane in it after all in the personalities of Ava and Oliver.

A few other interesting notes on the story. The berries from the baneberry plant are poisonous and can be deadly. Opinions vary on whether the rest of the plant is as toxic. Some literature states baneberry leaves will only make you sick while other sources report that all parts of the plant are deadly. For this book, I went with the latter option. English weddings do have their own unique traditions. I tried to capture a few of them for this book. When creative artists like songwriters and authors create art together they own the copyright to the music or book or poem jointly. Copyright lasts for the life of the author plus seventy years. So two people who write a song or book together are united in a way that will live longer than they will! Because copyright can be passed on to heirs, I thought the idea of two people at odds over some valuable content was an interesting angle for the mystery. You can see images of the places (real and imaginary) that inspired the novel at the *Death at an English Wedding* pinboard.

Thanks for stopping by Nether Woodsmoor with me. I hope you'll return there with me again soon! If you'd like more information about my other books, you can find my complete catalog at SaraRosett.com/books.

ABOUT THE AUTHOR

USA Today bestselling author Sara Rosett writes cozy mysteries. Her books are fun escapes for readers who like interesting settings, quirky characters, and puzzling mysteries. *Publishers Weekly* called Sara's books, "satisfying," "well-executed," and "sparkling."

Sara loves to get new stamps in her passport and considers dark chocolate a daily requirement. Find out more at SaraRosett.com.

Connect with Sara

www.SaraRosett.com

ALSO BY SARA ROSETT

This is Sara Rosett's complete library at the time of publication, but Sara has new books coming out all the time. Sign up for her newsletter at SaraRosett.com/signup to stay up to date on new releases.

Murder on Location
Death in the English Countryside
Death in an English Cottage
Death in a Stately Home
Death in an Elegant City
Menace at the Christmas Market (novella)
Death in an English Garden
Death at an English Wedding

On the Run
Elusive
Secretive
Deceptive
Suspicious
Devious
Treacherous

Ellie Avery
Moving is Murder
Staying Home is a Killer
Getting Away is Deadly
Magnolias, Moonlight, and Murder

Mint Juleps, Mayhem, and Murder

Mimosas, Mischief, and Murder

Mistletoe, Merriment and Murder

Milkshakes, Mermaids, and Murder

Marriage, Monsters-in-law, and Murder

Mother's Day, Muffins, and Murder

Made in the USA
Monee, IL
27 September 2020

43422077R00132